"Do you think I came here to trap you?" Cheyenne asked.

"No, I think you wanted to know if I was safe," Reese said. "You wanted a safe place to raise your baby. That's something we'll work out. But for now you're still my wife, and I'm going to help you."

She rested her hand on his shoulder. "You have to take care of yourself, not me."

"I have to take care of us both, or I might not make it through the next few months. Let me help you. You're about the only person in my life right now who makes me feel normal."

She placed his hand on her arm, and he couldn't think of anything better than that moment with Cheyenne. For now helping her took his mind off his own problems. He didn't for a minute think he was home free.

For the moment, though, he could still rescue a beautiful woman. A woman who happened to be his wife.

Books by Brenda Minton

Love Inspired

Trusting Him
His Little Cowgirl
A Cowboy's Heart
The Cowboy Next Door
Rekindled Hearts
Blessings of the Season
  "The Christmas Letter"
Jenna's Cowboy Hero
The Cowboy's Courtship
The Cowboy's Sweetheart
Thanksgiving Groom
The Cowboy's Family
The Cowboy's Homecoming

Christmas Gifts
  *"Her Christmas
    Cowboy"
*The Cowboy's Holiday
    Blessing*
The Bull Rider's Baby
The Rancher's Secret Wife

*Cooper Creek

BRENDA MINTON

started creating stories to entertain herself during hour-long rides on the school bus. In high school, she wrote romance novels to entertain her friends. The dream grew and so did her aspirations to become an author. She started with notebooks, handwritten manuscripts and characters that refused to go away until their stories were told. Eventually she put away the pen and paper and got down to business with the computer. The journey took a few years, with some encouragement and rejection along the way—as well as a lot of stubbornness on her part. In 2006, her dream to write for Love Inspired Books came true. Brenda lives in the rural Ozarks with her husband, three kids and an abundance of cats and dogs. She enjoys a chaotic life that she wouldn't trade for anything—except, on occasion, a beach house in Texas. You can stop by and visit at her website, www.brendaminton.net.

The Rancher's
Secret Wife

Brenda Minton

Recycling programs
for this product may
not exist in your area.

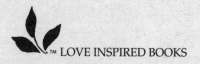

™ LOVE INSPIRED BOOKS

ISBN-13: 978-0-373-81639-2

THE RANCHER'S SECRET WIFE

Copyright © 2012 by Brenda Minton

www.LoveInspiredBooks.com

Printed in U.S.A.

Consider the ravens:
for they neither sow nor reap; which
neither have storehouse nor barn; and God feedeth
them: how much more are ye better than the fowls?
—*Luke* 12:24

This book is dedicated to my dad, Don Cousins, a Korean War veteran. March 1933–September 2011. And to all of the other brave men and women in our armed forces. Thank you.

Chapter One

The big white house with the pillars, the mul-tipaned windows, immaculate flower gardens and stone walkway were something out of Chey-enne's dreams. Who didn't dream of a house like this one?

Cheyenne Jones had a lot of dreams. Not many of them had come true. And instead of getting easier, things were getting harder. Maybe God meant to keep her holding on to Him by keeping her on her knees praying to get through each day? She didn't have much else to hold on to.

The only thing Cheyenne had was the 1982 piece of junk car sitting in front of this house and the memory of a man she'd met one time six months ago: Reese Cooper.

Weeks ago she'd gotten notice that he'd been injured in the line of duty. Now she stood on the stone path leading up to the big house belonging to the Coopers of Dawson, Oklahoma.

She guessed this was what true desperation felt like, standing in front of this home with her final paycheck in her purse and not much else. She'd felt all sorts of pressure in the past seven months or so. The first wave had led her to the altar. The second had led her here. In between, there had been small waves that beat her back, the way the ocean beat against the sand, a relentless pounding.

The door of the house opened. A woman stepped out, smiling. She looked to be about sixty, with light colored hair, a warm smile, a welcoming look. Cheyenne wondered how long she'd wear that look. Once she knew the truth, would she still smile? Cheyenne didn't know much about this family, the Coopers of Cooper Creek Ranch, but she knew that they were close. She knew that they were loyal.

They were everything she'd never had.

"Can I help you?" The woman walked to the edge of the porch.

"I'm…" Cheyenne breathed deep, past the tightness in her throat. The world swam a little, and she closed her eyes. When she opened them, the woman had moved down the steps and was walking toward her. "I'm here to see Reese Cooper."

"Oh." The woman stopped and held out a beautiful hand. "I'm his mother, Angie Cooper."

"I'm here to see…"

"I think you've already said that." Angie's smile faded, and her gaze lowered.

Cheyenne put a protective hand on her belly, and she bit down on her lip. "I'm Cheyenne."

It didn't register. Of course he hadn't told them. Why would he? Mrs. Cooper stared at her with a blank look, which meant Cheyenne didn't rate very high on Reese Cooper's list of priorities. Hadn't her mother always called her a silly girl? Silly because she'd always loved fairy tales, the kind where the handsome prince rides in on a big horse and sweeps the woman off her feet. Or kisses her and wakes her from a long and deadly sleep.

In her mind, Reese had become that prince— mainly because he'd given her hope that she'd never had. He'd made her believe that kindness still existed in the world. Strangers did wonderful and unexpected things. She'd fooled herself into believing she wouldn't always be alone.

She'd actually written him letters while he'd been deployed. He'd written back. They'd shared things—not like strangers share but the way a couple shares.

"Cheyenne?"

Cheyenne looked up, pulled herself back to reality and out of her fantasy world. The late July sun beat down on her, and the cotton of her shirt stuck to her back.

"Yes, ma'am."

"I don't think I know you. Did you go to school in Dawson?"

"No, I'm not from Oklahoma. I grew up in Kansas."

"I see. Did you meet my son in the military?"

"Kind of."

Angie Cooper sighed. "Honey, you need to tell me what's going on and how I can help you."

"If I could just see Reese." Her eyes burned, and she didn't want to cry. She didn't want to lose control. She'd cried way too much lately, and she'd decided on the trip here that the time for tears had come and gone.

That's about the only plan she had: to stop crying. Once she checked on Reese, she'd make her next plan. She'd decide where to go and what to do.

"I'm afraid he isn't here right now." Mrs. Cooper looked her over a second time—really looked her over.

Cheyenne should go. That's what Mrs. Cooper meant to tell her. Cheyenne wanted to agree. But where would she go? She closed her eyes as another wave of nausea hit, and her head swam. A cool hand touched her arm.

"Cheyenne?"

"I'm fine. You're right. I should go."

"I didn't mean that you should leave. And as pale as you are, I'm sure you shouldn't drive right now." Angie Cooper slid an arm around Cheyenne's waist. "Let's go inside and have a glass of tea."

They walked through the front door, paused in the entryway and then proceeded into the living room. Cheyenne thought she should take off her shoes or change into something nicer than the loose jeans and T-shirt she'd put on that morning at a gas station. She flicked her gaze across the living room with the pine hardwood floors, the overstuffed furniture and walls decorated with landscape paintings and family portraits.

This was the home of fairy tales, where happy people lived happy lives, loved each other, took care of each other. She allowed Angie Cooper to lead her from the living room, through a long formal dining room into a big, open kitchen. She told herself to stop the pity party, because her childhood hadn't been all bad. There had been love. It was conditional love, but love nonetheless.

Angie pointed to a big table that flanked one end of the kitchen. Everything in the house was big, made for a big family with twelve children. She felt like Jack when he climbed the beanstalk and landed in the giant's kingdom.

"Sit and I'll get that glass of tea. Have you had lunch?"

Cheyenne shook her head. Somewhere in the distance, a dog barked. Car doors slammed. Angie Cooper paused with two slices of bread on a plate and a slice of ham in her hand. She placed the ham on the bread and kept working. Cheyenne's stomach knotted and twisted.

"That's probably Reese. He's been with his grandmother." Angie Cooper brought the plate and a glass of tea.

"Is he okay?"

Angie's hand rested on Cheyenne's shoulder. "He will be."

The sandwich on her plate no longer appealed, even though her stomach had been growling for hours. From the front of the house, she heard the door close, a loud thump, an aggravated exclamation. Angie Cooper started to say something, but then she shook her head and walked away.

Cheyenne stood. "I shouldn't have come."

She'd waited too long. Reese Cooper walked through the door. An older woman in a pink suit stood next to him. The woman touched Reese's arm. He stood motionless in the doorway. His grandmother looked from Cheyenne to Reese, back to Cheyenne.

Cheyenne's vision blurred. She sat back down, thankful she didn't have food in her stomach as a wave of nausea assaulted her.

"Reese, you have company. Cheyenne is here." His mother moved toward him, her smile sweetly gentle—a mother's smile.

Reese stood silently and was as tall and handsome as she remembered, though not as clean shaven, and his sandy brown hair was a little longer. That day in the restaurant she might have fallen a little in love with him. He'd been so kind, a cowboy in jeans and a button-up shirt, his boots the real thing. He'd been no urban cowboy. She'd seen plenty of those in Vegas. He'd been a gentleman, sitting with her in a booth as she poured out her life story. In the end, he'd rescued her.

Cheyenne waited, thinking he should at least say something. They weren't strangers. He'd become a friend through letters he'd written—a dozen letters. She had them all in her one suitcase. She'd come here to make sure he was okay. She'd also come here because she had nowhere else to go and Vegas hadn't been the place to call home.

"Cheyenne?" Reese finally spoke, but he stared straight ahead, not turning to look at her.

Cheyenne felt her fairy tale crumble. This is what happened in real life. People got hurt. Heroes came home injured. Damsels stayed in distress unless they rescued themselves.

Mrs. Cooper's hand held her arm, but Cheyenne pulled away. He had to hear her heart breaking as she walked toward him. It thundered in her ears. Her vision clouded with unshed tears. She reached him and touched his hand.

"Cheyenne Jones." She drew in a deep breath. "We met in Vegas."

A tiny hand held his. Reese felt her warmth. He inhaled her scent. He remembered her letters. But what was she doing here? He stared at blackness and waited for clarity. His secret was that he kept waiting for vision to return. He kept telling himself the doctors were wrong and he'd see again.

But for two months he'd lived in darkness. Since the day an explosion had rocked his world, killed men in his platoon and left him blind, he'd been praying it was a dream he'd wake up from.

The last thing he'd been thinking about was the woman standing in front of him. Since the accident, he hadn't really thought about that day in Vegas or the impulsive moment when he'd told a crying waitress that he'd marry her.

"I'm sorry." Her voice was as sweet as he remembered. That's what had struck him about her—even then. She'd been leaving her job as a waitress, dressed for her evening job as a dancer and he'd seen a vulnerable young woman needing a break. He'd seen innocence in her eyes.

He could still hear that innocence in her voice. He smiled because he was sure that some people might not agree with him about her innocence. They would have looked at her life, her job and thought the opposite. He didn't mean to be poetic, but he had looked into her eyes and seen her heart.

And now she was here. He shook his head because he couldn't do this. He couldn't have her here, in his life.

"What are you doing here?" He spoke quietly, but the words were loud and echoed in the darkness, sounding harsher than he'd intended.

"I wanted to check on you." Her voice wavered. Next to him his grandmother mumbled that he had the manners of an ogre. She released his arm and told him he was on his own. He could handle that. He'd been coddled since the minute he'd walked through the front door a week ago. His grandmother had actually been the only one who didn't smother him. She'd told him to cowboy up and remember he still had a life—unlike the men in his platoon.

She hadn't said those words; they were his. But she'd told him he owed it to those men to live his life to the fullest.

"This was a mistake." Cheyenne's voice slipped away from him. He heard a chair move and heard her footsteps again.

He reached for her, but she wasn't there. "Could we have some privacy?"

Cheyenne stepped close again, bringing her scent: lavender and vanilla. "They've already left the room."

He reached, needing a place to sit down. A hand touched his arm, guiding him to the table where he felt the back of a chair. He smiled. "Give me a minute. I didn't expect you."

"No, of course you didn't." She pulled her hand loose from his. A chair scraped, and he knew she'd sat down across from him. "I got a visit from the military, someone checking on my welfare after you were injured. I wasn't the person to notify in case of emergency, but they saw that you were married and they sent someone to tell me about the accident."

Reese brushed a hand through his hair trying to make sense of how all of this had happened and what he should do. His wife of six months was sitting in his mother's kitchen, needing him. And he couldn't be the person she relied on. He had no hope of ever seeing again. His left arm and his spine had been hit with shrapnel, and walking still took everything out of him. What was he supposed to do for her?

She moved again. He knew she did because her scent brushed past him. He'd only known her for three hours, and he recognized her scent. He didn't know if it had to do with enhanced senses from losing his eyesight or because he'd memorized that scent while he stood next to her in a little wedding chapel in Vegas.

"I should go. I shouldn't have come."

He couldn't agree more. This hadn't been the deal, her showing up here. In any other life, it might have been okay, but in this new life, everything had changed.

"Where will you go?"

She sobbed a little, and he reached, found her arm. That day in Vegas he'd thought she was the prettiest thing he'd ever seen. Tiny, with light blond hair that hung wavy to her shoulders and big blue eyes smudged with mascara and tears. He'd been about to be deployed, and she'd needed someone.

"I'll figure something out. I have family, you know."

"Yes, family."

She'd told him bits and pieces about the parents who had turned their backs on her. She didn't really have family. She didn't have anyone. He took a long breath that hurt deep in his back and wished he could do more for her. "Cheyenne, I'll give you money. You have to eat and find a place to stay."

"I can take care of myself. I've been taking care of myself for a long time. I used the money deposited in my account to go to cosmetology school. That's what I always wanted. You gave that to me."

"So where will you go?"

"I'm not sure yet."

"I'll need your address." It seemed like a pretty rotten time to bring this up. "For the paperwork."

"I'll get it to you once I land somewhere." She kissed his cheek, and he was sorry he hadn't shaved in days. "Goodbye, Reese."

"The baby?"

"He's fine. It's a boy."

He smiled at that. "I'm glad."

She was already gone. He heard her walk through the house. He heard the front door close. And then he heard the light-soled steps of his mom walking back into the kitchen. He heard her hesitate at the door, but she didn't ask questions. He knew she had them.

"She's a friend. I met her in Vegas." He stood, unfolded the white cane he'd been learning to use and somehow managed to make it to the fridge without bumping into anything. Each day he got a little better. That's what the rehab experts had promised.

The counselor he saw each week told him he'd get past the anger, past the nightmares and the guilt. Cheyenne Jones somehow managed to be on the list of people he'd let down.

"Is the baby yours?" His mom stood behind him, her voice hesitant.

Reese turned, a glass of water in his hand. "No."

"Does she need help?"

He walked to the counter, feeling for it, finding it and then edging around to the bar stool he knew would be there. The first few days he'd had a few bumps and falls because people forgot

and left chairs out of place. They were learning.
He was learning.

"I don't know."

"Reese, this isn't like you. She's young. She's
here alone, and you let her walk out of this house
not knowing if she had a place to go or money
to get there?"

He brushed a hand through his hair and
leaned back in the chair. No, it wasn't like him.
He didn't know who he was anymore.

"I know. I'll work through this. I'll find her."
How?

"Do you need help?"

He got up from the chair, smacking the cane
against the side of the counter, looking for a way
out. "I'll take care of it."

"Reese." His mom hesitated.

He turned toward her, waiting. And she didn't
say anything. Because she didn't know what to
say? Or because everyone he knew was afraid
to say anything to him.

"Do you want me to go with you?" Heather
spoke from nearby. He shook his head. When
had his sister entered the kitchen?

He wondered if he would ever get used to
voices slipping through the dark. It reminded
him of a cartoon, a black screen and animals—
maybe cats—popping into the dark and then

fading again; laughing cats. That's how he imagined sounds, words. Nothing connected anymore. Everything was separate. There were sounds, words, touch, taste but nothing cohesive. Nothing made sense.

He raked his hand through his hair and wondered how bad he looked. He hated to shave, hadn't shaved in days. He knew his hair had grown out from the military cut he'd had two months ago. He wondered if he looked as angry as he sometimes felt.

"Reese?" Heather stepped close, touched his arm.

"I'm going for a walk." He took a few cautious steps and made it out of the kitchen. With the cane as a guide, he made it through the house and out the front door. And then what? He couldn't get in his car and go after her. He couldn't call her.

He couldn't see anything but black, and Cheyenne had left. The man he used to be was somewhere inside him, and even though he wanted to hide from this life, he couldn't.

Cowboy up, Reese. He could hear his grandmother's words, sharp, lecturing. How did a cowboy do that when he couldn't even get on a horse?

Chapter Two

Cheyenne left the Convenience Counts convenience store and turned right on a little side street with pretty turn-of-the-century homes and big lawns. She took a bite of the corn dog she'd bought and washed it down with a long drink of chocolate milk. She'd planned on going to the park that the owner of the convenience store had given her directions to. Instead she pulled her car up to the curb in front of a stucco building with a For Rent sign in the window. Across the big front window were faded red letters spelling out Dawson Barber Shop.

For a few minutes she sat in her car, staring at the building and daring to dream. She told herself to drive on, to forget this dream, to forget Dawson and Reese Cooper. In the end she opened the creaking door of her car and left it open as she walked up to the building and peeked in the window.

She barely had enough money for a hotel and a few meals. She needed a plan. She needed to decide where she would go and what she would do. The last thing she needed to be doing was looking at a building for a beauty shop.

An old bench had been left behind. It sat under a small awning. Weeds were growing up around it, sprouting from cracks in the sidewalk. Cheyenne sat down, scooting to the end of the bench, out of the hot July sun. She couldn't stay in Dawson. She had no one here, nowhere to go.

She could go home to Kansas. But then again, she couldn't. She couldn't face her parents now, not with all of the mistakes she'd made in her life. She couldn't face them because she'd been their problem, their mistake, too. Her birth mother had given her up. Her adoptive parents had given up on her.

But the biggest betrayal had been Mark's. Because after he learned she was pregnant he revealed that their marriage license wasn't real. He had no plans to be a husband and father. He'd laughed at her naiveté.

A little sparrow hopped around on the sidewalk, chasing bugs and dandelion seeds. She caught herself smiling as she watched him.

"Where do I go?" When she spoke, the little bird hopped back and looked at her. After his curiosity was satisfied, he plucked a dry bit of grass from the sidewalk and flew away.

She remembered a sermon from the church she'd started attending back in Vegas. That had been Reese's advice before he'd left that day. He'd promised to love, honor and cherish her. Then he'd kissed her, told her he had to go, but she needed to find a church. So she had.

One of the sermons had been about God's ability to care for people. If He provides for the birds who neither sow nor reap, how much more does He care for us?

She wondered if He knew that she was really at the end of her rope—hopeless. How had she come to this place in her life? She'd always had hope. She'd been the person in school who'd studied, thought about a future and how to be her best—until Mark and Vegas.

That showed how a couple of bad decisions could derail everything.

A car drove down the narrow road. It met another and had to pull off the pavement to let the other car pass. She smiled, remembering the town she'd grown up in. It had been larger than Dawson but had its share of narrow roads and pretty homes. A long time ago she had lived in one of those homes.

One of the cars, a long sedan, pulled in behind hers. Reese's grandmother stepped out of the car. She pulled on lace gloves and situated a white hat on her gray hair. She appeared to be a woman on a mission. And Cheyenne had a pretty good feeling that she was the mission.

Mrs. Cooper walked down the sidewalk and stopped when she reached Cheyenne.

"What in the name of all that is lovely are you doing sitting in front of this old shop?" Reese's grandmother dusted off the bench and sat down.

Cheyenne shrugged a little and blinked fast, trying hard not to cry. "Coming up with a plan."

"Well, if the bench works, so be it."

Cheyenne glanced at the woman next to her. "How did you know where to find me?"

"I prayed and asked God to lead me. He said to try the old barbershop. Here I am."

"God told you to find me here?" Cheyenne reached into her purse for a little package of crackers. She opened it and threw crumbs to the birds. "Really?"

The lady sitting next to her laughed…and laughed. Finally she wiped her eyes with a tissue she pulled from her pocket. "Land sakes, no. Before you start thinking I'm addled, I'll tell you. I asked Trish at the convenience store. Trish is nosier than me, and she watched you head this way."

Cheyenne smiled and shook her head. "I don't think you're addled."

"Most folks do wonder."

"Mrs. Cooper, I'm really very sorry about barging in and about Reese."

"Call me Myrna. Everyone does. Or Miss Myrna if you insist. But that does make me feel like I'm still teaching school. And you didn't do a thing wrong, coming to see Reese."

"I should have waited—or called him."

"Do you want to tell me what the story is between the two of you?"

"No, I'd rather not. I hope you don't mind."

"No, I don't mind. Young folks have a right to a few secrets. I'm guessing that isn't his baby you're carrying."

"No, ma'am, it isn't."

They sat for a few minutes. Myrna reached for the package of crackers and broke off a piece. She tossed it. The birds flew at each other, fighting over the little piece of cracker.

"Well, is there a father?" Myrna pulled off her gloves and pushed them into her little purse.

"Not to speak of." She shivered and looked away, at the golden sun peeking through dark green leaves of the trees in the lawn across from the shop. "Dawson seems like a good place to live."

"It is. I think everyone should live in Dawson. But then, I guess it wouldn't be Dawson if they did." Myrna twisted to look at the building behind them. "What is it about this shop that interests you?"

Cheyenne looked back at the shop. "I'm a beautician. I thought that someday I might rent a place like this and open a salon."

"In Dawson?" Myrna Cooper hummed for a minute. "Well, that's something we could use. So why don't you rent this building?"

Cheyenne stood because it was time to go. "I don't have the money. If I leave my number with you, could you pass it on to Reese?"

"First, let's take a look at this old barbershop. It was my uncle's, you know." Myrna reached in her purse and pulled out a key. "I happen to own it now."

Myrna stuck the key in the door, jiggled the handle and then pushed it open. "It's a mite musty after being closed up for the past couple of years."

"I like the smell." Cheyenne walked around the little rectangle building. It still had sinks, chairs—even a little room in the back and a bathroom. "But I can't afford it."

Myrna ignored her. She sat down in one of the plastic chairs near the window and smiled big. "I used to come in here with my daddy when I was a little girl. Back then Dawson had more to offer. We had a grocery store, a bank and a post office."

"I bet it was a wonderful place to grow up." Cheyenne smiled, but she had to sit down. Pain wrapped around her belly, and she breathed deep to get through it.

"Are you okay?"

"I'm fine, just a cramp."

"You're sure?"

She nodded and sat down in a chair near Myrna's. "I'm sure. I have a couple of months to go before I'm due. These are just Braxton Hicks contractions."

Myrna patted her leg. "Take the shop, Cheyenne. It's yours. I'll get the water turned on and the electricity."

"I can't. Myrna, I'm broke. Really, I can't."

Myrna Cooper stood and beckoned for Cheyenne to join her. "I'm going to help you do this. Young women should have dreams. They should have options. I don't know your relationship with my grandson, but I know if he could, he'd be the one here helping you. Until he can, you've got me."

"Oh, Myrna." Cheyenne closed her eyes for a brief "pull it together" moment.

Myrna touched her arm. "Let's go home. You can get a good night's rest, and tomorrow I think things will look better."

"'Home'?"

Myrna pursed her lips and widened her eyes. "My house, young lady. That's what I mean by home. Stay the night or a few nights with me. And then we'll see what we can do with this old barbershop."

Cheyenne considered saying no but her body ached. She was hungry and tired. To top it off, her car hadn't been running right. For the last few hundred miles she'd worried she wouldn't make it to Dawson. And where else could she go? Myrna Cooper seemed to be an answer to prayer.

After a few days of rest, things would look different. Maybe she could take Myrna up on her offer. This shop could be the place to start her new life. But how would Reese feel about her settling in his hometown? That hadn't been part of their bargain. He had never counted on her in his life for good—not even as a neighbor.

Reese sat on the front steps of his parents' home, letting Adam MacKenzie tell him what a great opportunity it would be for him to work at Camp Hope and how great it would be for the kids who attended. Reese held out his hand to the dog that brushed against him, licking his arm.

"Adam, I can barely help myself right now. I'm not sure how I could help kids who have been dealing with disabilities their entire lives. There are days that I'm pretty angry. I'm trying to be independent, but man, there are days. Try asking for help finding a pair of shoes. That'll teach you what humility is. I'm a grown man, and I have to ask what shirt to wear."

"Reese, you're honest. That's what these kids need, not someone who puts on a smile and pretends every day is perfect but someone genuine who can admit he gets angry."

"I'm not sure. Not yet. When I can make it through a day on my own steam, maybe then. Right now I'm afraid the kids would be helping me more than I could help them." He took the stick the dog pushed into his hand and gave it a fling.

"Reese, these kids are always teaching me something. That's part of the joy in this camp— what it does not just for them, but for us."

"I'll think about it."

Adam stood, touched his shoulder and walked away. "Pray about it."

"Will do."

Reese sat on the steps until he heard the car door close and the engine start. He waved and Adam honked. He stood and turned to go back inside the house. The dog returned with the stick. Reese took it one last time and gave it a toss.

"Hey, watch it." His sister Heather let out a shriek. "I'm down here, you know."

He laughed a little and stopped on the top step. "Sorry. And no, I didn't know. Are you going to town by any chance?"

Heather joined him on the steps. "Yeah, actually. I had to drop some artwork off with Jackson, and now I'm heading back to town."

Their older brother had gotten married while Reese was gone, and his new wife was redecorating.

"Yeah, but that would make more driving. You'd have to go in to Dawson, back out here and then home."

"Yeah, horrible, it might add six miles to my trip. Reese, I can drive you to town. Where do you want to go?"

"Rumor has it that Gran has moved Cheyenne into the barbershop."

"Not a rumor."

He unfolded the white cane that hung from his wrist. "I need to find out what's going on."

"Okay, let's go." She touched his arm. "How do you know her?"

He walked next to her across the yard. "I met her in Vegas."

The answer bugged him. She was more than someone he'd met. She deserved better than that. Unfortunately he didn't quite know how to give her better. He was still working on that. The situation between them would have been easy if he hadn't been injured, if she hadn't shown up in Dawson. The arrangement they'd made had seemed pretty cut and dried, until now.

"She's pretty." Heather spoke softly.

"Yeah, she is."

"She wears a wedding ring on a chain around her neck. Do you know her husband?"

The question dug for more answers. Rather than giving them, he opened the passenger door of Heather's sedan. "I used to."

The answer seemed to satisfy some of her curiosity. She got behind the wheel of the car, and they headed to town. Within feet of the driveway he was sorry he'd asked Heather for a ride. She was a challenge to ride with on a good day. When a guy couldn't see what was coming at him, she was treacherous.

"Maybe slow down for the curves." He reached for the handle above the door.

"I'm not that bad."

Not bad, his foot. Heather's driving encouraged quite a few "get me there safe" prayers.

She cleared her throat. "How'd rehab go yesterday?"

"I'm going to move back into the guesthouse." He said it in an easy tone and then waited for his sister's reaction.

It took a few minutes. "You what?"

"I'm moving back into the guesthouse." A few years ago he'd moved into the apartment over the unattached garage next to the main house. Since he'd come home, he'd stayed with his parents. "I need my own space."

"Are you sure that's a good idea?"

"Yeah, I think it is. I can't see, but I can still live my life. I'm going to start doing rehab and physical therapy here. They'll help me organize, label everything and even teach me how to keep my clothes together so I know what I'm putting on."

It didn't come easy, listing everything he needed help with, everything he'd always taken for granted. Walk to the closet, pull out clothes. Walk to the kitchen, pour a glass of... He no longer knew what he was pouring in his glass, and he'd never been fond of surprises.

"The clothing part is good. I'm not sure who dressed you today but…"

She laughed and he smiled.

"Thanks, sis, you're a help."

"I aim to please."

There were a few more minutes of silence and another sharp curve. "Do you mind stopping at the store? I've been given strict orders to get out more. Something about proving to myself that I can do these things on my own."

"Was there ever any doubt?" Heather said it as if there hadn't been doubts. He'd had plenty.

"A few." He leaned back and relaxed.

The car slowed, eased into a parking space, bumped the curb and stopped. He laughed because some things never changed. Their dad had been getting on her for that since she'd turned sixteen.

Heather's hand touched his arm. "You ready?"

"As I'll ever be." He reached, found the door handle and pushed.

When he stepped out of the car, he breathed in familiar scents. Molasses-coated grain from the feed mill, Vera's fried chicken at the Mad Cow Café and fertilizer on a nearby field. He stepped forward, white cane swinging and then hitting the curb. He stepped up, wondering where Heather had gone to.

He could hear hammering down the block and a truck leaving the feed store across the street. He turned, took a step and waited.

"You coming with me?" Heather finally spoke.

"Of course." A grown man shouldn't have so many hang-ups. He could walk into the convenience store and get something. Even if it was just a pack of gum, he could do this.

His therapist had told him he had to take these steps because the longer he hid at the ranch, the harder it would be to leave. So he walked down the sidewalk, his hand resting lightly on Heather's arm for guidance.

"We're at the door." Heather had stopped.

"Okay. So the next step is in." He wondered if she was as nervous as he was. He drifted back on the memory of Cheyenne in Vegas and standing next to her at the altar. They'd both had sweaty palms, and he'd felt her tremble.

He hadn't thought about it much, but it took a lot of desperation for a person to hitch themself to another person that way. Maybe they'd both been a little desperate.

"Here we go." Heather stepped away from him and pushed the door open.

"Right. Here we go." Before stepping through the door, he had another question. "Is Trish in there?"

"Staring. About to head this way."

"Point me in the right direction."

She did, and he walked away from his sister because she would run interference with Trish. The cane swung, hit metal. He reached and touched the end of the rack. Candy. Mints. Gum. He'd been here enough times in his life that he knew what each aisle held—unless Trish had remodeled, and she never had before.

"Reese Cooper, how are you?" Trish called out from behind him, loud, as if it was his hearing that had been lost.

He considered shouting back. Instead he smiled, picked up a plastic container of mints and turned toward the counter. "I'm great, Trish. How are you?"

"Really good. And it is so good to see you out and about." She continued to talk loud and clear.

"It's good to be out."

Trish pushed buttons on the cash register. "That'll be a dollar."

He pulled his wallet out of his pocket, felt the bills and handed the appropriate one to Trish. "One dollar."

"Well, now that's pretty amazing." Trish spoke with such admiration he couldn't be mad. "How'd you know this is a dollar?"

"It's a new skill I've learned. Thanks, Trish."

He pocketed the mints and walked out of the store. Heather followed.

"Do you want to walk across the street or drive?" She pulled him to a stop. "We're at the edge of the sidewalk."

Reese nodded. "We can walk."

He had to stop stalling and face Cheyenne.

"Fine. Let's go."

A car honked. He stepped back. Heather reached for his arm. She took a step forward, and he followed her lead.

"Okay, we're across." Heather stopped, and he stopped with her when the cane hit the curb.

"What's all the hammering?"

"Roofers. Gran said this old building needed some help."

"This has been going on for the past few days, and you all thought I wouldn't find out? Because secrets are so easy to keep in Dawson."

"A woman we don't know, a pregnant woman, showed up in Dawson looking for you. That kind of puts us all on the defensive."

"The baby isn't mine, and she isn't after anything."

He loved it when the Coopers circled the wagons. But now wasn't the time for wagons to be circled. True, he didn't know Cheyenne much better than the rest of them, but he knew she wasn't there to use him. He knew because he had come to know her through the letters she'd sent while he was in Afghanistan. He knew.

Heather sighed and stepped forward. "One step up and we're on the sidewalk."

"Trust me." He leaned close to her. "I'm a big boy."

"I know you are. But who is she to you? That's all we really want to know."

If he knew, he'd probably tell her. At the moment, he didn't know who Cheyenne was to him. He knew what the paper said. He knew the plan, but somehow it had changed.

Reese reached, touched the door and turned toward his sister. "I can take it from here."

"Reese, we're trying to…"

"I'm good." He pushed the door open and stepped inside. Heather didn't follow him. He smiled, because he knew he could count on her. She'd give him time. She'd wait for him. He took cautious steps forward, the cane swinging right to left. It hit a chair. He stopped to listen.

Then he heard a thump against the back wall.

"Cheyenne?" He took more careful steps.

Silence—and then the hammering he'd heard from across the street. It echoed inside the building. At the back of the room he heard footsteps. He smiled and laughed a little.

"I know it's you."

"Okay, it's me." The voice, soft and tremulous, drew closer. "What are you doing here?"

"I could ask you the same question. Funny thing, my family all seemed to know you were here. I'm the only one in the dark, so to speak." He smiled and reached, finding a chair. He sat down. "I hope you don't mind if I sit."

"Go right ahead."

"You're still in town." He folded the cane. "I thought you left."

"I thought I would leave, but I didn't have anywhere to go. I was sitting on the bench out front when your grandmother found me."

"Be very careful of my grandmother. She loves matchmaking. It's her gift." He smiled and turned, trying to find her. She had moved. He heard soft footsteps getting closer.

"I'm not here to be matched to anyone. I'm here because I needed to know that you're okay."

"There's more. I can hear it in your voice."

"That's your imagination." She sat down next to him, lavender and vanilla. He leaned a little toward her because he couldn't see her and he wanted some connection with her, some way to know she was there.

"No, it isn't my imagination. I'm very good

at voices. It's because I can't see. They say it enhances the other senses."

"Really, and what does my voice tell you?"

"I hear strain. And you hesitate each time you tell me you're fine. See. I'm very perceptive."

"I'm not trying to hide anything from you. I just don't want you to think that I came here expecting more from you than you've already given me."

"I want to help if I can." He reached for her hand.

"You've helped so much, Reese." She squeezed his hand. "You don't owe me anything else."

He stood because she had. "I have to disagree, Cheyenne. I think I owe you for better or worse, in sickness and in health."

"Those are vows for real couples who have real weddings. That isn't your promise to me. Your promise to me was your last name and life insurance if something happened to you. Because of you I have insurance and I had money for school."

"What do you know? Something did happen to me."

"I'm sorry." Her voice cracked, and he felt like the creep Heather sometimes said he'd become. "I'm sorry that something horrible happened to you. But I'm going to have a baby. I don't have a family I can turn to. And I want to stay here."

"Cheyenne, you don't have to leave." He reached, found her hand and pulled her close, but she wouldn't step into his arms.

"I have to make a life for myself and my son. I want to be somewhere safe. I want a community. A neighborhood where kids play and ride bikes."

"You'll do great here." He backed up a step and put the distance between them she seemed to want—distance he probably needed. "Do you need anything?"

"No, nothing. I'm good."

"If you do need help, let me know."

"I'll let you know." She walked him to the door. "Reese, I can be here for you, too. If you need anything at all. Even if it's just a friend."

"Thank you." He shrugged as he reached for the door. "I'm still trying to figure out how to take care of myself."

"You're doing better than you think."

He smiled at her optimism. "That's good to know."

"Reese, about the annulment. We should get that taken care of."

"Soon."

As he walked out the door, Heather waited

for him. He heard her move, felt her hand on his arm. "Ready to go?"

"Yeah, thanks for waiting."

"Watch out. This sidewalk is pretty broken up in places." She placed his hand on her arm, and they walked in the direction of the main road. "Step down, and we'll cross the street."

"Gotcha."

"Reese, do you want to talk?"

"Not yet, but thanks. I've got to figure this one out on my own."

It wasn't simple because he wasn't the man he used to be. He definitely wasn't the man Cheyenne needed in her life. Cheyenne needed and deserved a man who could take care of her. She deserved a real marriage.

The plan to dissolve their marriage had seemed easy back in Vegas. Now that he knew her, knew the food she loved most, the colors that made her happy, the music she listened to when she was down—all of the things she'd shared in her letters—it didn't feel like an easy in-and-out plan.

Chapter Three

A few days after Reese's visit, Cheyenne sat down in the barber chair and looked at the shop, at her dream. She smiled and rested her hands on her belly. She'd cleaned and polished, and the only thing left to do was paint. She would wait until she talked to a doctor before she undertook that task. She wanted to make sure it would be safe for the baby.

She eased out of the chair and headed for the back room. What had once been a storeroom was now her little apartment. It held a bed, a chair, dorm-sized fridge and microwave. She even had a tiny bathroom and a closet. It wasn't much, but at least she had a place to stay, a place of her own.

The bell over the door jangled. Cheyenne stepped around the corner and peeked out. Heather Cooper stood at the front of the shop looking at the pictures on the wall. Cheyenne wiped her hands on her jeans and straightened her top. Those adjustments didn't make her feel any more confident, not with Heather standing in the front of the little shop, looking completely together in linen capris and a pretty top of soft fabric in summery blues and greens.

Years ago Cheyenne had been a lot like Heather, before mistakes that turned her into a different person, someone she didn't recognize. Living in Dawson, she thought maybe she'd find the old Cheyenne. The old Cheyenne knew how to smile and greet Heather.

"Heather, it's good to see you."

Heather turned from the photographs in black and white of customers who used to patronize the Dawson Barber Shop.

"The pictures bring back a lot of memories. I know most of those men." Heather smiled and walked across the room. "How are you?"

"I'm good. Getting settled and trying to get work done so I can open soon."

"What else do you have planned?"

Cheyenne looked around the barbershop, and she shrugged. The room was long and narrow. There were molded plastic chairs at the front of the building, midway back a counter with a couple of bar stools. The old barber chair sat between that and the back wall. Opposite the barber chair there were a couple of sinks for washing hair.

"Not much really. Maybe paint the walls."

"What colors?" Heather walked around the room, as if it was a normal day, normal conversation.

Cheyenne stood in the center of the room and watched the other woman. It wasn't a normal day. They weren't friends, although Cheyenne wondered what that would be like, to have someone like Heather to talk to, to have coffee with.

Cheyenne shrugged in answer to the paint color question. "I don't have a clue."

"I'll help if you'd like. And if you want my opinion, I think decorate with the photographs and the past in mind."

"That's a great idea. But I couldn't ask you to do that."

"Consider it my 'welcome to Dawson' gift." Heather took a seat on one of the stools behind the counter, and Cheyenne knew this had nothing to do with the shop or welcoming her to Dawson.

"That would be a wonderful gift, but you don't have to." Cheyenne stood for an awkward moment, and then she sat next to Heather.

After a few minutes of silence Cheyenne shifted to face her guest. "Why are you really here?"

"Cheyenne, I want to know about you and my brother."

Cheyenne breathed through a pain that wrapped around her middle, and she wanted so badly to tell Heather to leave, to let it go.

"I'm not going to give you information that Reese hasn't given. This is between the two of us."

And what would people think of her if they knew the deal she'd made with Reese Cooper? Would they be as welcoming as they'd been? Would Vera at the Mad Cow still welcome her with pie? Would Myrna Cooper ask her to leave?

Sometimes she didn't know what to think of herself.

"I'm sure it is between the two of you." Heather shook her head. "He's my brother, and I don't want him hurt."

"He isn't going to be hurt."

Heather gave her a careful look and then she nodded.

"When he's around you, I see pieces of the old Reese. No matter what the situation is between the two of you, I think you're good for him."

"I'm the last thing Reese needs in his life. He

has a wonderful family, and he's going to get through this." Cheyenne rested her hand on her belly. "I'm here to start a life for my baby and myself. I'm here because Reese told me stories about this town, the people. That's all, Heather. There's nothing more between us."

"I'm not so sure about that." Heather hopped down from the stool. She grabbed her purse, and she smiled an easy smile. "I'm busy the next two days, but I'll be back Thursday to help you. And if you're interested in church, Dawson Community Church is at the edge of town."

"I'd love to go to church. But about the decorating—I really can't afford to pay you."

"I'm not asking you to pay me." Heather stopped at the door. "And if you need anything, let me know."

Cheyenne nodded and managed a smile. After watching Heather drive away, she went back to her room and sat on the edge of the bed. Another pain wrapped around her belly. She'd been having them all day, these pains. She'd timed them. They weren't regular, but she still didn't think it should happen this way, not this often or this soon.

She should find an emergency room—alone. She closed her eyes and leaned back, giving herself a pep talk. She could do this. She didn't have to call someone. She didn't need anyone to hold her hand. In two months she would be a single mom with no one to call or lean on. She'd made the decision to have this baby, and she could do this.

Alone.

She closed her eyes and let one tear trickle down her cheek—only one. She wouldn't let the rest squeeze out. She was done crying. She had a life to get hold of, a baby counting on her. She picked up her purse and left, locking the door of the shop behind her.

Fifteen minutes later she pulled into the parking lot at the emergency room for the Grove hospital. She sat for a second, telling herself she'd been imagining the pains. But another hit as she sat there. She breathed through it and then got out of her car and headed toward the entrance of the E.R. As she walked through the double doors, a receptionist smiled a greeting. The woman, gray-haired and kind, told Cheyenne to take a seat and she'd get her information.

Cheyenne pulled out her insurance card and driver's license. She handed both through the window to the woman who took them, then looked at Cheyenne over wire-framed glasses.

"You just moved to town?" The woman, her name tag said Alma Standish, asked.

"Yes, ma'am."

"You'll need to find an obstetrician very soon. We have a couple here in town." She peered at the insurance card and shook her head before handing it back. "I'll have our nurse get your vitals, and then we'll get you right back to the E.R."

"Thank you."

As if on cue the door to the E.R. opened and a nurse peeked out. "I can take you back. We'll get your blood pressure and temp."

Cheyenne picked up her purse, thanked Mrs. Standish and followed the nurse back to the E.R. The nurse, wearing blue scrubs with teddy bears, pulled a curtain and motioned Cheyenne into the small cubicle.

"You can sit up here." The nurse helped Cheyenne onto the exam table. "How many weeks?"

"Thirty-two."

"Okay, has everything been normal up to this point?"

Cheyenne nodded and held out her arm for the blood pressure cuff. The nurse listened, wrote down information and started to walk out of the room. The curtain slid back, and the doctor walked in, staring at the chart in his hands. He looked up, black wire-framed glasses on a straight nose. His dark hair was a little long.

"Cheyenne Jones Cooper?" He read the name from the chart and then looked at her, clearly puzzled.

The nurse shrugged when he looked at her.

"Yes." She cleared her throat at the weak answer and tried again. "Yes."

"You didn't list a spouse. Is there someone we can call in case of emergency?"

She shook her head. "No, not really. I'm fine, though."

"I'm the doctor. I'll decide that." He helped her lay back on the exam table. "Cheyenne, I think you should know that I'm Jesse Cooper."

She moved to sit back up. "I should go."

"Not so quick. We have an obstetrician who happens to be in the hospital. I've called her down to examine you. And now is there someone I should call?"

"No, there's no one."

"But you're married to a Cooper?"

"It isn't…" She shook her head and blinked back tears.

Jesse Alvarez Cooper pulled tissues from a box and handed them to her. "It's okay."

But he didn't sound as if it was okay. She remembered back all those months ago when Reese had told her about his family. Jesse had been adopted from South America. Reese called him overly serious and said he had no sense of humor.

He was the last person she needed to run into today. Unfortunately, he didn't seem to be in the mood to let her leave. And the sudden wave of nausea that hit was a good reason to wait and see the doctor.

Reese lifted the weight one last time and set it on the floor. He stretched and then rolled his shoulders to loosen the overworked muscles.

"The end. I'm done."

He grabbed the towel off the back of the rowing machine and draped it around his neck. The only thing he wanted now was the recliner and a glass of iced tea. Jeff, the physical therapist, a guy from Tulsa, laughed.

"We're not done."

"Really, I thought we were. My body feels pretty done. You know, I have an idea. Tomorrow let's go riding."

"We'll definitely try that in the next few weeks. I need you to step on the treadmill now."

"Yeah, okay." He'd never thought he'd be sorry his dad had put a gym in the basement years ago. Tim Cooper had thought a gym would be a way for rowdy teenagers to work off energy and stay in shape.

The door opened and someone walked down the stairs. He paused before stepping on the treadmill. His parents were in Grove. His brothers Jackson and Travis had hauled a load of cattle to an auction. The footsteps were soft-soled—not boots—and heavy, so it wasn't one of his sisters. He smelled men's cologne, not cow manure.

"Hey, Jesse." He grinned and really wanted to pat himself on the back. Instead he stepped on the treadmill and waited for Jeff to turn it on.

"Nice game and you're right." Jesse's voice stopped close by.

Reese raised his hand for a high-five. Jesse ignored it.

"What brought you over? Was the sun shining too brightly, acting a little too cheery for you?"

"Your bedside manner leaves a lot to be desired." Jesse said it with a hint of humor. "I'm turning this off. We need to talk."

"Make it quick. I have a nap calling my name." The treadmill stopped. He pulled the towel off his neck and wiped his face.

"Yeah, I don't see a nap in your future. So how's physical therapy going?"

"Great. Two hours today. But that isn't why you're here, is it?"

"No. But first I have to tell you I can't give you confidential information on a patient."

"I didn't ask you to, and why would I want information on any of your patients?"

"It isn't just any patient. Yesterday we had a young woman at the E.R. I called in a consult with our obstetrician."

"I see. And this pertains to me why?"

"Because her last name is Cooper, and rumor has it, she's paid you a visit. So I thought perhaps you'd want to know because you might want to drop by and check on her."

"Jeff, can we end this for today?" Reese reached, touched the table and found his bottle of water. "I promise I'll work twice as hard next time."

"Sure, Reese. Take it easy. And I can let myself out."

"Good deal. See you in a few days." Reese stood in one place and tried to visualize the gym. There was a bench by the stairs. He took a few steps, found it and sat down. Jesse sat next to him. "So you think you've connected the dots."

"I've been told my IQ is pretty high." Jesse let out a sharp breath. "And it might be because she has our last name and her previous address was Las Vegas—a place you happened to visit some time ago. After that it was careful deduction going through the list of brothers. Lucky is married. So are Travis and Jackson. I'm not and neither is Blake. Who would want Dylan and Gage? Brian is out of the country. That leaves you. And from the look on your face, I'd say you haven't told anyone that our mystery visitor is your wife."

"I'd like for you to keep this between us for the time being."

"For the time being, I will. When are you going to tell the family that you're married?"

"I don't know." He sucked down another drink of water. "We're not staying married. So maybe the fewer people who know the better."

"Why not?"

"It's…"

Jesse groaned. "Please do not say it's complicated. You've married a woman who is pregnant. She's acting scared to death, like someone might find out she's your wife."

"We had an arrangement." He stood and Jesse did the same. "Are you going to town?"

"I'm going back to my place." Jesse had a nice house on the lake. Reese had the feeling that big old house got pretty lonely sometimes.

"Could you drop me off at the barbershop?"

"That I can do." Jesse touched his arm. "Two steps and then the first step up."

"Thanks." Reese reached the stairs and grabbed the handrail.

They were on the road before either of them spoke.

"So how did you end up married?" Jesse finally asked.

Reese wondered if the word *married* really fit his situation. There had been a wedding. He'd even kissed the bride. But then he'd taken her back to her apartment, and he hadn't seen her again until she showed up in Dawson.

"She needed a break, Jess. She was pregnant, no one to lean on and flat broke."

"She isn't a puppy, Reese."

"I'm pretty sure I know that." He fiddled with the cane, folded and in his hands. "The father of the baby wanted her to get an abortion. And she considered it but then couldn't go through with it."

"That's pretty rough."

"She needed a break, someone to give her a chance to do the right thing."

"Do you have any feelings for her?"

Reese leaned back and rubbed a hand across his jaw. The truck slowed and made a right turn. Did he have feelings for Cheyenne? He admired her. Few women could pull themselves up the way she had. She'd used the money he'd given her to better her life. She'd packed up and moved across the country looking for a fresh start. She was having a baby alone.

"I'm not sure." That seemed to be the safest answer at the moment. Because how crazy would he be if he told his brother he might have feelings for Cheyenne? Because she had written him funny, touching letters while he'd been in Afghanistan? She'd shared the pregnancy with him: the first kick, the morning sickness and being upset that she couldn't fit into her jeans after the fourth month. Those letters had put him front and center in her life.

He knew that she felt rejected by the family that adopted her. She saw herself as their mistake, the kid they wished they hadn't adopted. She'd been rejected by the man she thought she had married.

The truck slowed again. "We're almost there. So do you have a plan?"

"I'm going to make sure she's okay and see if I can help."

Jesse cleared his throat. "I meant future plans for the two of you."

"The plan was to get an annulment when I got back." He didn't have much else to say. "Are we there?"

The truck slowed, and he heard the click-click of the turn signal.

"Turning now." Jesse cleared his throat. "Don't worry. She's going to be okay. So is the baby."

"Thanks." Reese reached to unclick his seat belt.

The truck slowed to a stop. "Do you want help getting in there?"

"No, I think I can handle it if you can give me a few directions." He reached for the handle and pushed the door open just a little. "And keep this between us for now. I don't care about myself. I don't want her to be hurt."

"I understand." Jesse touched his arm. "I parked right in front of the door, parallel to the curb. Get out, take three steps forward and you're going to step up. Ten steps and you're at the door."

"Is she here?"

Jesse laughed a little. "Yeah, she's here."

"What's so funny?"

"She looked out the window, and I think she's madder than Mia the day we sold her dolls at a yard sale."

Reese had pushed the door open. Now he hesitated. "That wasn't a fun day." A day they pranked their little sister and ended up grounded.

"You've got that right. I have to go, so see you later, little brother."

Reese stepped out of the car, closed the door behind him and took three steps. He touched the curb with his cane, stepped up and walked to the front of the building. Jesse had given perfect directions. He found the door and pushed. It didn't budge. He could hear Jesse's truck pulling out on the road.

He knocked on the glass of the door. No one answered. Great. He knocked again and pushed. It was still locked. He touched his pocket to make sure he had his cell phone. If she wasn't in there, he was going to hurt Jesse.

After a few minutes of knocking and getting no response, he eased down the sidewalk to the bench he knew used to be there. He couldn't stand up much longer. The bench was still there. He touched it and then sat, stretching his legs in front of him.

It turned out that in July heat sitting on that bench, even in late afternoon, felt pretty uncomfortable. Even in athletic shorts and a T-shirt, he was roasting. He would knock one more time, and if she didn't come out, he'd call someone to come and get him. Before he could move, he heard the door click and then open. He remained in one place, waiting, wondering if she'd try to play a game and slip past him. As she walked out the door, he spoke.

"Marco."

She didn't say anything. He tried again. "Marco."

There was no answer, so he smiled and tried charm as he stood to face the direction where he knew she had stopped. "You know, when I say 'Marco,' you're supposed to say 'Polo.' I'm not sure why it's Marco Polo but you get the rules of the game, right? I'm blindfolded and I say 'Marco.' You say 'Polo,' and maybe I can find you."

"I don't think those are the rules." Her voice reached him from a few feet away—soft, sweet, maybe a little teary.

"Why did you lock me out?"

"Why are you still here?"

"Because I'm nothing if not gallant. I've been told all my life that I'm a real Sir Gala. What was his name?"

"Sir Galahad? I'm not sure that fits."

"I could be Marc Anthony, and you could be... Isn't his wife a famous singer?"

She laughed a little. "I think they broke up, and I think that you definitely won't win points for pop culture or history. Marc Antony and Cleopatra would be the couple you're thinking of, and I've always thought she was tragic and vain."

He took a few steps and reached for her. Her hand touched his. "I think you're not vain. Actually, you don't realize just how beautiful you are."

"Neither of us is tragic, so we can't be Cleopatra and Marc Antony. Or the other two."

"Could we be Desi and Lucy?"

She laughed at that. "That's more like it. Why are you here?"

"Because you need me." He stepped close, feeling her breath, hearing her sigh. Her hand touched his cheek. It seemed like an invitation, so he leaned, touching his forehead to hers in an easy gesture. "Because I love being needed."

"I don't need anyone. I can do this. My needing you wasn't part of the bargain. I'm supposed to have this baby and then we get an annulment. End of story."

"I know it wasn't part of the bargain, Cheyenne, but if you haven't noticed, things have gone south in a big way. I don't think this was part of the bargain, either." He pulled off the sunglasses he wore and shoved them in his pocket.

"You have beautiful eyes." She sniffed a little,

and he wished those eyes worked so he could see her.

"I'd say, 'the better to see you with, my dear.' But that line is so cliché."

She sobbed a little and then her fingers touched his hair. "You need to shave. And your hair is too long."

"Are you going to stand here and point out all of my physical faults?" He reached, found the door and pulled it open. "I'm here to rescue you, and all you have are complaints. Wife, enter this building at once."

"Please stop."

He took hold of her hand, and he led her into the building. "Don't cry, Cheyenne."

"I'm so afraid."

Once they were inside the building, he pulled her into his arms and held her, the way he'd wanted to hold her a few days ago. They were strangers, friends, husband and wife. He'd make sense of it all later. The one thing they had in common was they were both afraid. "I know. And I'm here."

She nodded against his shoulder and repeated what he recognized to be her mantra. "I can do this on my own."

"I know you can. And I'm here to tell you that

I can help. I want to help. You need to sit down, and I'm going to make sure you're okay."

"Your brother told?"

She led him to chairs at the side of the room, and they sat down side by side. "He didn't tell me. He just hinted that my wife might need me."

"I'm sorry he found out. I didn't realize he would be at the hospital when I went."

"I'm glad you went. I'm glad he was there. But he didn't tell me anything. It's up to you to do that."

"It's nothing really." She released his hand. "I've had contractions. I thought at first it might be Braxton Hicks."

"Braxton who? Is he another Shakespearean hero? Competition for my affections?"

"False labor."

"Oh, that's a word I understand."

"But they monitored me for a few hours and realized they were real contractions. When I rest, they do go away, but they're real. The bigger problem is that my blood pressure is high."

"So what do we do?"

"I, not we. I'm not on bed rest at this point. I'm on medication and I'm taking it easy. I go back to the doctor in a week. And the obstetrician said to come in immediately if I have contractions that won't stop with rest, if I feel dizzy or experience serious swelling or headaches."

"'Taking it easy'? Is that what this is, remodeling a building? Do I smell paint?"

"I had help."

"What were you doing when I got here?"

She shrugged. He felt her shoulder move, brushing his arm. "I was putting up mini blinds."

"I'm going to help you, and then we'll call Vera and ask her to deliver something for dinner."

"You don't have to."

"I'm here, Cheyenne. I'm going to be here, and there isn't a lot you can do about that. You came to Dawson, remember?"

She stood and he heard her moving away. "Do you think I came here to trap you?"

He unfolded the cane and followed her voice. "No, I think you wanted to know if I was safe. You wanted a safe place to raise your son. That's something we'll work out. But for now you're still my wife, and I'm going to help you get this shop ready and make sure you don't have that baby two months early."

"I can't let you do that." She rested her hand on his shoulder. "You have to take care of yourself, not me."

"I have to take care of us both, or I might not

make it through the next few months. Let me help you. You're about the only person in my life right now who makes me feel normal."

A long silence and then she stepped close. "Can you use a drill?"

He laughed. "Can I use a drill? Of course I can."

She placed his hand on her arm, and he couldn't think of anything better than that moment with Cheyenne. For now, helping her took his mind off his own problems. He didn't for a minute think he was home free. Tonight he'd have more nightmares. Tomorrow he'd feel frustrated and useless. Next week he'd have a good day and think he could conquer the world.

Today he could rescue Cheyenne. He covered her hand with his. "Where's that drill?"

Chapter Four

"Drill?" Cheyenne hesitated because she'd forgotten mini blinds. She'd forgotten about taking it easy. Her gaze had lingered on the face of the man who, on paper, belonged to her—her husband.

In Vegas he'd been the one person who'd told her she could do this pregnancy thing. She could make it work, and she could keep her baby. Cheyenne thought about the birth mother who chose to have her. She still wondered about that woman, what her situation had been.

Her hand rested on Reese's arm, and he looked down, as if seeing her, seeing her hand. But his hazel eyes didn't focus, didn't see. She wanted to touch his face, let her hand rest on the strong line of his jaw and touch the raspy stubble of his unshaved cheek.

Break contact, a little voice whispered into

her mind. She needed to step away, find a focus point other than her husband's face, his strong shoulders and the way it felt to have his hand on hers. She moved.

"I'll get the drill," she whispered, a little hoarse.

He walked behind her, staying close to her side, stopping when she stopped. She wanted to back away. Instead she closed her eyes and took a deep breath. His hand touched her back.

"Did you find it?"

"Yes. Now what?" She picked up the drill.

"Well, you get the parts we need and then we measure so that we get the blinds even." He touched her arm. "Sit down."

"I have to help."

"No, you don't. You have to give your baby a chance to make it to term." He reached for the drill, taking it from her hand. "I really can do this. Or at least part of it. You sit and give me directions, and I'll see what I can accomplish."

She nodded and moved away from him.

"One important rule, Cheyenne." He cleared his throat and she turned. "You have to tell me what you're doing. I can't see you walk away or see you nod your head. I can't even see a frown, so I don't know when I'm on thin ice."

Heat slid up her cheeks. "I'm sorry. I'm getting what you need, and I'll be right back."

"Thank you." He smiled an easy smile. "I'll wait over here."

She watched him unfold the cane he used and walk to the window to wait for her. He sat on the windowsill, his muscular legs clad in black shorts. He wore a white T-shirt that contrasted with his deep tan. She looked away, hurrying to grab the tape measure, pencil and other items she'd left on the bed. When she returned he smiled again, this time less confident—a little boy smile on a man's face.

Shy? Or unsure?

"Here it is." She gave him an inventory of what she had and put it all on the folding table near the window, along with the drill and the parts for the mini blinds.

"Thank you. And now you sit down."

She did as he ordered, sitting on one of the old plastic chairs that had probably been in the building since the 1950s. They were faded yellow and orange and not at all comfortable. She wouldn't get rid of them, though. They were a part of the past, like the black-and-white photos on the wall. They connected her to this place, made her feel as if it had become her history, her town.

Reese measured the inside of the window using his hand to make sure the space was the same distance down on both sides. He then tacked a small nail in place. She didn't know why but she didn't question.

"So tell me something about yourself that I don't know." He smiled as he reached for the brackets that would attach to the wall.

"Not a lot to tell."

"Were you a shy child or outgoing?" He held up a package of screws. "And I need four of these for each end. Could you find the right ones for me?"

"I can." She took the plastic package from his hand. "I was shy. I never quite…"

She found eight matching screws and handed him four.

"Never quite?"

"Nothing."

He didn't turn away. Instead he stepped closer, and then he brushed the seat next to her with his hand and sat down. "Never quite what?"

"Not now, Reese."

"You aren't going to make this easy, are you?"

She smiled because he smiled, disarming her, making her think that they could really be friends if given a chance. "My sister was born when I was five. Surprise! All of a sudden I was the child they shouldn't have adopted. They should have had more faith in God. They should have waited for Melissa."

His expression softened, and he shook his head. "I'm sorry they made you feel that way."

She knew he meant it. Of course he did. But she also knew that he probably had some similar feelings about marrying her. He'd married her on impulse. Someday the right woman would come along, and he'd be sorry he'd rushed ahead of God and married her.

"I'm sure they didn't mean to." She whispered the words for fear saying them too loud would bring an onslaught of tears that she couldn't control.

"Is that why you went to Vegas?"

She closed her eyes and fought emotion that tightened her throat. The baby kicked against her ribs, and she touched her belly, letting her hand rest where her baby fought for space inside her. She breathed deep.

"I just wanted to…" To be loved. Unconditionally.

"You wanted?" His voice was soft—raspy soft.

She breathed deep again, this time to get through a pain that tightened around her belly. "Could we let this go?"

"I think we can. Have you called them lately?"

"No. Reese, they don't want to hear from me. I was their mistake. They adopted me when I was six months old, and they regretted it for the next seventeen years."

"I don't know how they could regret having you."

She stood, needing space, needing to breathe deep. "Don't you regret telling a dancer in Vegas that you would marry her?"

He blinked a few times and then shook his head. He stepped away from her, moving carefully to the other side of the window where he placed a small nail in place to mark where the bracket would go. After he'd tacked it in, he turned. "Where did that come from? We were talking about your family, and now it's about us?"

"Reese, you have to regret. This isn't what you expected to come home to. This isn't the life you expected."

"Maybe not, but it's the life I have and I'm going to meet it head-on."

Defeated, she sat back down. "How? How do you meet this head-on?"

"How else would I meet it, Cheyenne? And I know you're stronger than this. You're not a quitter."

"I don't know anymore. I'm just not sure how to get through each day."

"With faith."

She squeezed his hand. "I'm not sure if I have enough."

"Then we'll get each other through the next few months. We'll survive this."

"And then, after those months are over? Then we go our separate ways. No regrets."

He let go of her hand and walked back to the table where she'd set the hardware for the mini blinds, and he didn't respond to what she'd said about regret. Maybe he already regretted.

"First we tackle these mini blinds." He picked up the drill and the screws she'd given him earlier. "The rest will be a piece of cake."

She wanted to agree, but she couldn't. For him, maybe it would be a piece of cake. He had a big family surrounding him, helping him to get through his situation. He had faith he'd been relying on since birth. He'd never been anyone's mistake—not even hers.

Reese mumbled something about the drill. She watched him hold the tiny metal piece to the window, butted up against the nail he'd put in place as a marker. With his free hand he reached for the screws on the ledge.

"Let me." She reached for the screws and held

them out to him. Realizing her mistake, she put one into his hand. "I'll get the drill."

"You have to admit, we make quite a pair."

"We are definitely a pair." She handed him the drill, and he held it up, wincing. She reached but stopped short of touching his arm. "We don't have to finish today."

"The more we get done, the less we have to do later."

He squeezed the trigger, driving the screw into place. He took the next screw from her and made quick work of it. After all four were in place he stood back, flexing his shoulders.

"Now I think I'm done." He rubbed the back of his neck and shook his head. "And done in."

Cheyenne stepped to his side and ran her hand down his back. He flinched, but he didn't move. "Thank you for helping."

"You're welcome. And that feels good." He leaned his head forward.

She ran both hands down his back, massaging the tightness from the muscles. Slowly he turned, his hands finding her arms and then sliding around her. He pulled her close.

"Cheyenne." His right hand came up to cup her cheek. She closed her eyes as he brushed her cheek with his fingers. Slowly he moved forward until his lips were a breath away from hers. His mouth moved against hers and she sighed. He kissed her long and easy, retreated for a brief moment, then returned as if tasting her a second time.

She came to her senses first, pulling away, breathing deep.

"We can't do this." She rested her hand on his cheek, wanting nothing more than to be in his arms but knowing it couldn't happen like this. They both needed…

They needed strength. They needed someone to hold them. They needed space—and time to think. They didn't need more to regret.

"You're right." He stepped back, felt for the windowsill and sat. "I'm sorry."

As much as she agreed, those were the last words she wanted to hear him say. But she accepted them. She had to or she'd cry.

Reese sat for a second, getting his bearings, thinking through the moment when he'd thought it would be a good idea to kiss Cheyenne. Maybe he did it because he needed something that felt a little normal, like life before Afghanistan, before the accident.

Cheyenne deserved better than that from him. He had come here to help her, to show her they could be friends and that she had someone to count on. He hadn't come here to make things uncomfortable between them.

He opened his phone, and a computer voice told him the time. He didn't care about the time; he needed those few seconds to get his bearings. Only feet away, Cheyenne exhaled and then he heard a chair move, the metal legs scraping the floor.

"Are you okay?" He couldn't see her expression. He didn't know if she was in pain, upset, angry, sad.

"I'm good." Strain. Tears?

"Are you?" He needed more. And maybe she needed an apology. "I really am sorry."

Because she didn't need this. She didn't need something else to worry about, someone else to take care of. For ten years she'd worked two jobs while Mark gambled everything away and left them living in one-room apartments at old motels.

He stood, still waiting for her answer, still wishing like everything that he could see her face. For more reasons, he realized, he needed to read her expression.

"Please, don't be sorry. I'm not sure that sorry makes me feel better, Reese. It kind of sounds like you're sorry you kissed me." She laughed a little and he smiled. That's what he had first noticed about her. Even when she'd fallen apart in his arms at that diner in Vegas, she'd found little things to laugh about.

He smiled and moved to the chair next to hers. "I'm definitely not sorry about that kiss. But I'm sorry for putting you in a place where you have something else to worry about. We need to focus on keeping you healthy and keeping that little guy safe until he's big enough to come into the world."

She sobbed and her head leaned against his arm. "I'm so pathetic. I'm afraid. I'm not sure what I'm going to do."

"It's going to be okay." He pulled her close. "We're going to get through this. And I'll be here for you."

"I don't want you to feel like I'm your responsibility."

She was his responsibility—for better or worse. He'd made vows that day in Vegas. He just hadn't planned on this turn of events, for her to be here in his life. He hadn't planned on her needing more from him.

"I'll call Vera's and have something delivered." He switched to a neutral topic, and she relaxed against him.

"You don't have to do that."

"Yes, I do. Do you have any other furniture?

These chairs can't be what Jesse means when he says take it easy and keep your feet up."

"I'll put my feet up later."

And he knew when to let something go. "What do you want to eat?"

"A salad would be good."

"A salad with what type of meat? I'm new at this, but I think you might need protein."

"Grilled chicken then and ranch dressing." This time he heard the smile in her tone, and he smiled back. Yeah, he could still be someone's hero.

After ordering, he slipped the phone back in his pocket and waited because he didn't know what to say and Cheyenne didn't seem to be talking.

"Are your parents upset?" Her question a few minutes later took him by surprise.

"About my blindness?"

"No. Are they upset about me showing up here?"

"I don't think so. Why would they be?"

"Reese, did you tell them that we're married?"

Oh, that. It seemed a little hot in the barbershop. It was probably the sun coming in the big windows at the front of the building. He thought about mentioning that and how the blinds would help. Instead he answered with the truth. "No, I haven't. It's hard to find the right time to break the news."

"I see."

Silence fell between them again. Reese didn't know what to say. How did he explain that in marrying her he'd chucked about a lifetime of convictions out the window? He'd been the Cooper least likely to play the field, most likely to find the right woman and put a ring on her finger. He'd taken one moment in Vegas, the tears of a pretty woman, and he'd tossed it all.

What would his family think when he broke the news that he'd married a stranger? A pregnant stranger. The two of them had gone to a chapel where they'd rented wedding attire, found a few witnesses, and he'd bought a pretty ring from a selection in the front office of the business.

The wedding business. He shook his head when he thought about that day and how right it had felt to walk down the aisle with a woman he'd bumped into outside a diner. He laughed a little, and next to him, Cheyenne cleared her throat.

"What's so funny?"

He turned toward that voice, the same voice that had shakily repeated after the minister that she would be his lawfully wedded wife, to have and to hold. He reached for her hand.

"I was thinking about our wedding day. You have to admit it was pretty crazy."

"'Crazy'? Do you think that word is strong enough? I walked into you, fell apart and married you. All on the same day."

He smiled at the memory. "We did like the same pie. That seemed to be a sign."

"Right, coconut cream without meringue."

"Calf slobbers," he corrected. "Meringue looks like the slobber from a bottle-fed calf."

"And that's still gross." She rested her hand on his arm. "Reese, I can do this on my own. We could get the annulment now, and your family would never have to know."

"Your son is going to be born in two months. We're not backing out on our deal. I'm not backing out." He held out his hand and her fingers slid through his. "Remember our dinner after the wedding?"

"Oh yes, our reception at the casino seafood buffet. You invited a dozen people we didn't know to eat with us. And then you made sure I got home safely."

"Not exactly the happy ever after that fairy tales are made of." He felt a real need to apologize, which was crazy. "We didn't even kiss goodbye."

"We aren't really married, Reese."

"I know."

The bell above the door dinged. He stood, surprised by sharp pain down his back. Physical therapy and installing blinds all in the same day might have been too much. He didn't want Cheyenne to know. Yeah, he had his cowboy pride.

He reached into his pocket and got his wallet out.

"Hey, Reese."

The voice sounded familiar. He couldn't put a name with it.

"Hi." He pulled out a twenty. The bill was folded in threes to keep him straight. "Keep the change."

"Thanks. I'll set these on the counter." She continued to talk. "You all enjoy."

And he remembered. Mary Stanley.

"Thanks, Mary."

"You all have a good night." She walked away, her voice fading as the door closed behind her.

"Dinner is served." He turned, wondering where Cheyenne had gone to.

She touched his arm. "I'm here."

"You're okay?"

"I'm good."

He reached into the box that had been set on the counter and pulled out two plastic containers and then two drinks. He held one out to Cheyenne, and she took it from his hands.

They sat together at the counter. He remembered years ago when Uncle Johnny would sit on these same bar stools behind this counter, talking to one or the other of the old-timers who used to get their hair cut. He'd gotten his hair cut here.

"Could you tell me where the mashed potatoes are?"

Her hand touched his and guided it. "Three o'clock. And salad is at nine o'clock."

"Thank you. We make a pretty good team, don't we?"

"Reese, we aren't a team. We don't have an 'us.' We have to figure out what do with this."

"'This'?"

"Our lives. Me, the baby, you…"

"Blindness?"

"No." She sighed. "Maybe. It's time to be serious. This isn't a marriage. It's an arrangement. There's a reason you haven't told your family about me. I'm not the girl they always thought you'd bring home."

At least she was honest—tough but honest.

He slid his hand across the counter, found her arm and squeezed lightly. And he didn't say anything because he didn't have an answer, and she knew it. She didn't need games from him.

He'd learned an important thing being a middle kid in a family with a dozen children. He knew when to keep his mouth shut. He knew when to let the woman have the last word.

"I think we shouldn't tell them." She finally spoke.

He turned toward her. "Why is that?"

"Because we're not staying married. They don't have to know. We can be friends and end this after the baby is born. That was the plan to begin with."

"No harm, no foul."

"Right."

"No one gets hurt."

"Exactly." Her voice wavered. He sighed.

They finished eating in silence. After the last bite, he stood, holding the closed plastic container. "If you direct me to the trash, I'll throw this away. And then if you don't mind, I could use a ride home."

She took it from his hands, and then she returned and slid her arm through his. "I'll drive you home."

A few minutes later they were bumping and

bouncing down the road in her car. Reese listened to the engine and shook his head. "You're going to need a new car soon."

"I can't afford a new car."

"I'll get the keys to my truck. Someone should be driving it."

"I can't take your truck, Reese."

He sighed, suddenly exhausted. "What if I let you use the truck and in return you drive me to Tulsa when I need to go. If you do that, we're helping each other."

For a long time she didn't respond. The old car rattled up the driveway and chugged to a stop. "I'll think about it. And we're here."

He held out his hand, and she put hers in it for a brief second. He let go and opened his door. When he got out, she was waiting for him.

"You don't have to walk me to the door."

"I don't mind." She took his hand. "But I'm not kissing you good-night."

They both laughed, and he pulled her a little closer. "What if I kiss you good-night?"

"Please don't. Not tonight." The smile faded from her voice, and she stopped walking. "We're at the steps."

He released her and unfolded the cane.

"When you get back to the shop, you need

to rest. And I'll stop by tomorrow to check on you."

He felt a soft movement, air shifting past him, and he knew she'd stepped close again. "I have to do this on my own."

"You need to let people help you."

"I can take care of myself. I have to take care of myself." She touched his arm only briefly. "Goodbye, Reese."

He nodded and walked up the steps. The front door opened. He smiled and stepped through.

"Reese," his mom greeted him. "Was that Cheyenne?"

"We'll talk later." When he knew what to say, when he knew what he was thinking.

Chapter Five

On Sunday Cheyenne drove to the Dawson
Community Church and sat in the parking lot.
As the lot filled, she watched people walk to the
church. They walked in groups, laughing and
talking, sharing stories. She sat alone, unnoticed
in the far corner. For ten years she'd lived outside of this lovely part of society. She thought
about the few friends she'd had in Vegas—
showgirls, waitresses and one or two who had
jobs that would have really made the good citi-
zens of Dawson blush.

How did she go from who she had been in
Vegas to someone accepted in Dawson? How
did she walk into this church, wearing a sec-
ondhand or maybe thirdhand maternity dress
and sit with these people who looked as if they
had always belonged?

She sat in her car through what should have

been Sunday school. She waited until the bell rang, signaling the beginning of the service, and finally she worked up the courage to get out.

The church bell rang a few more times. Cheyenne loved that sound. It meant something constant, unchanging and holding to tradition. She wanted each of those things. She wanted real faith, constant, unchanging. She wanted something to pass down to her child. She wanted her little boy to always know that he belonged, that people wanted him.

To get what she wanted she had to walk through the doors of that church, face the people inside, their stares, their whispers and their speculation. She had to pretend Reese Cooper meant nothing to her. This had to be about her, about God and her unborn child.

Before she could make it to the church, she saw him. He walked down the steps, the white cane hanging loosely from his hand. Heather stood at the top, watching. She waved before stepping back inside, leaving the two of them alone. Reese reached the sidewalk and faced her, his smile easy, his eyes hidden behind sunglasses.

"Cheyenne?" He took a few steps in her direction.

"Yes."

"Heather saw you. She doesn't usually come here on Sundays but today is Dad's birthday." He stopped, and she walked up to him, taking his arm and turning him toward the church. The gesture came easy—too easy. It seemed as if they'd always been.

"I nearly chickened out," she admitted as they paused at the bottom of the steps.

"You're still shaking." He slid his hand down her arm to lace his fingers through hers. "They really don't bite. God doesn't send bolts of lightning."

"The roof doesn't cave in?"

"It's never even cracked. Wait, once. But that was because of a tornado."

"Good thing." She swallowed and then took a deep, fortifying breath. "I'm ready."

It had been easier in Vegas. The church there had been filled with people like herself, people seeking answers, forgiveness, acceptance. But then, maybe people everywhere were seeking those same things.

"I'm not letting go." Reese leaned to whisper close to her ear.

She smiled at that and thought he probably would let go. Eventually. They walked up the steps. He took it easy, right foot first, holding the rail and sighing when they reached the top.

"Sometimes it feels like mountain climbing." He spoke quietly as they walked through the doors.

"I know." Not physically, but emotionally, spiritually, she knew about climbing mountains. "Can we sit at the back?"

"Not on your life." He held tight to her hand and leaned to whisper. "The Coopers always sit in the second pew, right-hand side. There are twenty pews. I count to nineteen, and we're home."

He touched the back pew, number twenty, and each step he took, he reached to touch the pew and she knew he was counting. When they reached his family, he motioned her in first and then he slid in next to her.

Around her she heard a flurry of quiet whispers, and she knew people were talking. The speculation continued. She wanted to stand up and shout that yes, she'd done things she was ashamed of. And yes, she'd married Reese Cooper at a wedding chapel in Vegas. But she loved God and she loved…

She closed her eyes and gave herself and the people around her a break. She knew that speculation wasn't the worst thing. People were going to talk. Curiosity couldn't be helped.

The choir stood to sing and Cheyenne stood

with the congregation. The song was about falling down before God. And she wanted to but in private and not here, leaving people to speculate more, to question her sanity. And she did question it herself...often.

Throughout the service she listened, got distracted. Her thoughts were spinning, and the man next to her didn't help. He stared straight ahead, a slight smile on his face as he listened to the preacher. Every now and then he shifted in the seat, stretched or leaned close. His hand remained on hers.

Church ended. Everyone stood. Cheyenne stood. Reese moved out of the pew, taking her with them. People pushed around them, closing in. She wanted to leave, but the hand on hers held tight.

"Reese, who is your friend?" A man walked up, his smile genuine as he looked from Cheyenne to Reese.

"This is Cheyenne. She just opened up Uncle Johnny's old barbershop."

"You're a barber?" The man's brows drew in. He hitched his thumbs through the straps of his bib overalls.

"A beautician, actually. But I can cut a man's hair, too."

"Well, I'll stop by and give you a chance. It'd save me driving to Grove."

"Yes, sir."

"Don't call me sir. The name is Hank."

"Hank. Thank you."

Her heart slowed its nervous pace as more people stopped by to meet Reese's "friend." Reese held her hand, and with each introduction, her confidence grew and she thought maybe she'd make it here. Maybe she'd be able to come to this church, raise her son here and find friends that accepted her.

Maybe she'd learn to be okay with herself. Because hadn't the sermon been about just that? God created us, and He didn't make mistakes. He always had a plan. He was like the voice on the GPS, urging us to turn around at the earliest convenience, to get back on the right path. And at the end of the journey, the voice informed, "You have reached your destination."

She needed a destination to reach.

Another hand touched her arm. She turned and smiled into the clearly questioning eyes of Angie Cooper. The look didn't hold anger or resentment, just questions. And Cheyenne couldn't be the one to give the answers. For the last ten minutes, as they'd made their way to the door, Reese had introduced her as a friend, nothing more.

It might be for the best if they kept it that way. Then when things ended, there wouldn't be questions. Explanations wouldn't be required. They could continue to be friends.

Besides, she wasn't his wife, really.

"Would you like to join us for lunch?" Angie smiled a genuine smile with the invitation.

Lunch with the Coopers? She hesitated, lost a step and tripped over nothing more than carpet. Reese grabbed her up. "Careful."

"Sorry, I'm more clumsy lately."

"Have you been feeling okay?" Angie held her other arm, and together they walked out the door and down the steps.

"Yes. I've stayed off my feet and taken the medication. Things seem to be better. The doctor Jesse sent me to seems to think I'll make it to term if I take it easy and rest as much as possible."

"That's good advice. And if there's anything we can do, please let us know."

"Thank you, Mrs. Cooper." Cheyenne looked around, looked for a way to escape because she couldn't spend the day with this family, pretending to be someone she wasn't, wishing she was someone she wasn't.

"Lunch?" Reese stood next to her. When she turned to look at him, her ability to reason clouded over.

For a brief moment she looked at him, her husband, and she wanted to keep him. She wanted to keep his smile, his hazel eyes, the comfort of his touch. He stood there, unaware of the way her eyes misted over. He didn't know that her heart hammered an unsteady rhythm each time she looked at him. And today, standing there so tall and straight in jeans and a pale blue button-up shirt, today he looked like someone she could love.

If love even existed....

"I have to go." She touched his arm. She smiled at Angie Cooper. "I really have to go."

"Cheyenne?" Reese followed after her. "Not fair."

"I'm sorry." She stopped on the sidewalk, twenty feet away from him. "I can't do this today."

"I know." He said it quietly, somehow keeping it between them.

With that, she left. She hurried to her car, started the fussy thing by pumping hard on the gas and somehow got out of the parking lot without hitting anything.

She considered not stopping. If she kept

driving, she would land somewhere. She could start over in any small town. It didn't have to be Dawson. This should have just been a stop, not a stopping place. She could have checked on Reese, seen that he was okay and moved on.

One bag was all she had to pack—one bag. It was all she had to her name. She had one bag, no one to turn to and no one waiting for her to come home.

The house smelled like roast and fresh bread. Reese eased down the stairs, going slow because there were nieces and nephews here for Sunday lunch and they had a bad habit of leaving things on the steps or tossed around the living room. Last week he'd stepped on someone's favorite doll, nearly doing in the doll and himself in one fell swoop. It was another reason for moving back to his apartment. It was much safer, fewer obstacles.

"Hey, what's up?" The loud voice came from the bottom of the steps. A lesser man would have screamed like a girl when that voice came at him out of the dark.

"Nice, Mia. Maybe next time use a bullhorn."

She laughed, of course. "Stop being so sensitive, and give me a hug."

And then her arms were around him, squeezing tight. His sister happened to be nearly his height when she wore those crazy heels of hers. To top it off, her arms were like bands of steel around his middle.

"Maybe try not to crack my ribs." He gasped and managed to escape. "Where have you been for the past couple of weeks?"

"Staying close to Tulsa. Did you miss me?"

He had, actually. "No way."

"Liar."

"Probably. So help me get to the kitchen without breaking my neck."

"Are you sure you want to go to the kitchen?" she leaned close and whispered.

"Do I not want to go to the kitchen? I smell roast and bread."

"Yes, but can the inquisition be smelled?" She had hold of his arm. "Watch out, Barbie at twelve o'clock."

"Good thing you came along when you did. Barbie and I would have had matching broken necks."

She stepped away from him, and when she came back, her hand touched his, stopping him from moving forward. "You're doing okay, right?"

"Of course I am. Eyesight is so overrated."

"Don't do that, Reese. Don't pretend this is okay with you."

"It isn't okay with me. But what do you want me to say? I lost my eyesight. Guys in my unit lost their lives." He was at home, surrounded by family. The families of those guys were struggling to come to terms with the fact that their soldiers wouldn't come home.

"It wasn't your fault."

He patted the hand that rested on his arm. "I know and I'm surviving."

"Have you thought about talking to the other families? Maybe the Bernard family, in Oklahoma City. They're close enough to drive to."

"What would I say to them? Sorry your son didn't come back home and I did?"

"Maybe, if that would make you feel better."

"It wouldn't. Could you tell me what the inquisition is about so I can prepare a defense before I get in there?"

"Someone named Cheyenne."

"Gotcha."

"Reese…"

"Mia, let it go." They were in the living room, and he proceeded with caution through the room. There could be toys—or someone listening.

"Is she important to you?" Mia pulled him to the left. "Barbie parked her car in the path."

He managed to laugh. "Barbie is out to get me."

"She's been hanging out with G.I. Joe."

"That's how it starts."

"And she's important to you?"

"Barbie?" He shrugged. "No, not really. She's a doll but really not my type."

"Cheyenne, and stop deflecting. You of all people should know better."

"Physician heal thyself? Or person with the major in psychology and counseling, counsel thyself? Of course I should know better. And she is important, but that's all I plan to say."

Mia stopped walking. Reese turned to find her. "I'm here for you, big brother."

"I love you, Mia, and I'm good. So let's get this over with."

"It's your life." She giggled a little and reached to put his hand on her arm.

From the dining room he could hear conversation in the kitchen. He heard his name mentioned. Someone mentioned Cheyenne. Mia cleared her throat, loudly. He laughed a little at her lack of subtlety. Mia had never been subtle. She'd been Mia Nunez until she'd turned eight and became a Cooper. Her life had been rough, scraping to survive basically on her own. She still knew how to take care of herself, but the rough edges had been softened. She painted and illustrated children's books in her spare time. She was a DEA agent and had a black belt.

"We're coming in, so if this conversation is going to happen, I'm going to be a part of it." Reese made the announcement as they walked into the kitchen. "And I'd like for everyone to leave but Mom and Dad."

He heard footsteps, whispers and then silence. He smiled and laughed a little at the rapid exit. "Are they gone?"

"They're gone." His dad walked past him. "Do we need to sit down?"

"If you want." He leaned against the counter, needing to stand up. He heard chairs scrape and knew his parents had decided to sit.

"I heard you're moving back into your apartment. Are you ready for that?" His dad spoke from a short distance away.

"I think so. I have to do it sooner or later."

"I think that's good." Tim Cooper was beating around the bush.

So much for the plan to keep this marriage between Cheyenne and himself. It would have made it easier. There would be less mess if they ended it quietly without everyone knowing and having an opinion. But this was his family. They didn't hide things from each other. They worked together and helped each other through the hard times. And he knew that if Cheyenne needed them, they'd be there for her, too.

But where did he start? He guessed the best course of action would be to get it over with, jump right in with the facts.

"Cheyenne Jones is Cheyenne Cooper." He drew out the words, waiting for it to sink in.

"How in the...?" His dad stopped. "What does that mean?"

"She's your wife?" His mom's tone said a whole lot.

"Yes, she's my wife."

"Well, this isn't what I expected." His dad cleared his throat and then chuckled a little. "How did this happen and when?"

"In Vegas before I went to Afghanistan."

"Were you...?"

He shook his head, knowing what his dad wanted to ask. "This isn't what you think. The baby isn't mine. Cheyenne and I didn't have a fling or anything else that comes to mind. She needed help, and I offered to marry her."

"You married a complete stranger because she needed help?"

"She was pregnant with no one to turn to. I didn't know what would happen to me in Afghanistan. It seemed like a good way to help her. She could be on my insurance and be my beneficiary if something should happen to me."

"And what was the plan for when you came home?" Tim Cooper no longer sounded amused. Reese turned toward his dad, wishing they could make eye contact, wishing he could read his dad's expression. Maybe he didn't want to see the disappointment, though.

"The plan is the same as it was when Cheyenne and I made this arrangement. After the baby is born, we'll get an annulment."

"That's it? You think it will be that simple to sign a paper and push this young woman from your life?" His dad's tone said as much as his expression would have. Reese sighed.

Simple? No, he no longer thought it would be that simple. In Vegas they'd been strangers who'd happened to meet and make a bargain. Now? He had to admit that Cheyenne could no longer be counted a stranger. She'd stepped front and center into his life. It had started with the letters she'd written him—funny and sweet, a little bit sad. She'd managed to touch him with her stories.

"I hadn't planned on her being in my life." He needed a glass of tea and a minute to get his head on straight.

"Can I get you something?" his mom asked as he walked through the kitchen.

"I can do it." He found a glass and then turned to the fridge for ice. "I can get a glass of iced tea. I can take care of the situation with Cheyenne. I want her to be able to stay here and build a life for herself when this is over. I want her to be accepted and cared for by the people in this family."

He turned, touched the pitcher of tea on the counter and poured it in his glass.

"We'll do what we can for her." His mom walked up behind him and hugged him for a brief moment. "We're all here to help."

"I know. That's why I'm telling you. She doesn't have family, and she's going to need our help."

"Reese, don't rush into this annulment."

That came out of left field. "Mom, it's a marriage in name only."

"Is it, Reese? Because I think you took vows even if you didn't mean them. Even if you were thinking temporary, maybe God had another plan in mind."

"I can barely take care of myself. I'm pretty sure I can't take care of a wife and child."

"Now what?" His dad approached, leaning against the counter next to him.

"I'm not really sure. I didn't have this part planned out. There were no contingency plans. It was either I don't come home and she gets the life insurance or I come home and we get an annulment. End of story."

"Nothing is ever as simple as we think it will be." His dad patted him on the back. "I know you'll do the right thing."

He nodded and left the room. For now the only right thing he knew was that Cheyenne needed time and he needed space. He walked out the back door and across the yard to the garage and his apartment.

Chapter Six

What in the world? Cheyenne ran to the window of her shop and looked out. It had been a peaceful Tuesday morning in Dawson when out of the blue she'd heard screeching tires and honking from several directions. Glancing toward the intersection, she saw the problem. A car in the middle of the road turned cockeyed like the driver had decided at the last minute to make a turn.

Cheyenne shook her head when she recognized the car. She grabbed her phone and her purse and hurried out the door and down the sidewalk. Myrna, tall and elegant, stood next to her car giving the other driver a tongue-lashing. When she saw Cheyenne, she smiled a little and leaned against the car as if the fight had suddenly gone out of her.

"Myrna, are you okay?" Cheyenne took hold

of the older woman's arm and eased her into the car. "Here, sit down."

"I'm fine, really." She leaned a little and put her hand up to whisper, "Always play on their sympathy."

"I see." Cheyenne managed to not smile as she stood and turned toward the man walking toward them, weaving between the cars. His eyes had narrowed and he studied Myrna.

"Is she okay?" He shot a look from Cheyenne back to Myrna. "Myrna, you all right?"

"I do feel a little faint, Larry."

"You almost sent us both to the hospital." He shook his head and exhaled loud and long. "What were you thinking?"

"Well, Larry, I guess I wasn't. I'm old, you know."

Larry laughed a loud, barking laugh. "Myrna, that ain't gonna work with me."

"Was there any damage?" Cheyenne asked the other driver, a farmer in work jeans and a faded button-up shirt.

"No, but someone needs to call Tim Cooper and tell him to get that woman off the road."

"I'm not *that woman,* Larry. You know my name. I ran you out of my garden when you were knee high to a grasshopper. I'll take a switch to your backside right now if you don't run too fast."

Larry grinned a little and shifted the toothpick sticking out of the corner of his mouth. "She decided to turn at the last minute. I didn't hit her, but I came pretty d—"

"Don't you use that language around a young lady!" Myrna shouted. "That's my granddaughter you're talking to."

Larry gave Cheyenne a careful look, and Cheyenne shot a look in Myrna's direction. "I'm not her granddaughter."

"Close enough." Myrna sighed and settled herself back into the driver's seat. "Let me get this car out of the road before people start talking and saying I've lost my mind."

Larry shook his head and backed up a few steps. "Take it home and park it, Myrna."

"I'll do what I please, Larry."

"I'll drive you, Myrna." Cheyenne waited, and Myrna slid to the passenger side, allowing Cheyenne to get behind the wheel.

She glanced in each direction and pulled across the street and down the road to the barbershop, now the Dawson Barber Shop and Salon. She pulled next to the curb, the passenger side close to the door.

"I love the new sign." Myrna nodded in the

direction of the window. "Dawson Barber Shop and Salon. Very nice way to keep tradition. Thank you for that."

"Myrna, I owe you the thanks, not the other way around."

"Well—" Myrna shook her head and sighed heavily "—I owe you for getting me out of that jam. I don't know what came over me. I just decided at the last minute that I didn't know which way I wanted to go."

"You forgot?" Cheyenne's heart thudded hard against her chest. Myrna cackled and patted her arm.

"Don't look at me like that. No, I didn't forget. I just wasn't sure where I wanted to go, and at the last minute I decided to come here and check on you. Jesse stopped by my place the other day after dropping Reese off here."

"Oh, I see. And he told you?"

"Not a word, but Jesse isn't the cool character he sometimes thinks he is. He purposely closes himself off, but I know he's worried about his brother and he's concerned about you."

"I'm not your granddaughter."

Myrna opened her car door. "Honey, we both know that isn't true. Just give Reese time to come around. He always does the right thing."

"Myrna, this isn't his baby."

"That doesn't matter to a Cooper." Myrna stepped out of the car, and Cheyenne followed her to the shop that she, of course, hadn't locked. She was starting to believe no one ever locked a door in Dawson.

"Do you want tea?" she offered as she and Myrna stepped into the cool interior of the building.

"My goodness, that paint smell could curl a gal's hair without a perm. No, I don't want tea. I want to know if you've got family you need to call. There might be people wondering where you're at."

"I doubt it."

"Why, honey, if you were my girl, I'd want to know that you were safe."

"Myrna, that's because you're a Cooper. I haven't talked to my parents in ten years."

"Then I think it is high time you did." Myrna walked around the salon, touching the high counter, the plastic chairs, the pictures on the walls. "So many memories. Some are nearly as faded as these pictures and the plastic of the chairs."

"But they're good memories."

"Yes, mostly good." Myrna turned to face Cheyenne, her smile a little less vibrant, her hazel eyes soft with tears. "You need to call your parents. I promise you that holding on to bitterness won't make you any happier. It'll just break your heart and theirs. Take it from an old lady who knows."

Cheyenne sat down and Myrna sat next to her. "What happened, Myrna?"

Myrna stared toward the front windows, but Cheyenne thought the older woman wasn't seeing the glass, the street, the dog walking behind a little boy. She didn't see a summer day in Dawson. After a minute, she smiled a smile that didn't reach her eyes.

"I had a daughter, years ago." Myrna's soft voice wobbled a little. "She left home when she was eighteen because she didn't want this silly old town or this small-town life. We thought she was making a mistake, but she wanted to be an actress."

"I'm sorry."

"So am I." Myrna looked away but not before Cheyenne saw tears fill her eyes. "She never came back. We talked a few times on the phone, and we tried to tell her we loved her and understood that not everyone stays in the town they were raised in."

"What happened?"

Myrna patted Cheyenne's arm. "She got killed in a car accident in Los Angeles."

Cheyenne wrapped her arms around Myrna. "I'm so sorry."

Myrna nodded and wiped at her tears with a tissue she pulled from her purse. "It's in the past, but it still hurts like crazy. You think about calling your parents. It's real easy to say you'll do it tomorrow. And then tomorrow becomes next week, next month, next year. Don't put off making amends with people who love you."

Cheyenne nodded, and at that moment, hearing Myrna's pain, she couldn't delve into the reality that she didn't know if her parents loved her, not the way Myrna had loved her daughter. She didn't know if they missed her or even cared that she'd left. She hugged Myrna again, and Myrna sniffed a few times and stood.

"I have to get home to my doggies." Myrna patted Cheyenne's cheek. "You take care of yourself. Rest like the doctor said. And do what I tell you, because I'm old and smart."

"I will." Tomorrow.

Myrna smiled as if she knew. "Today."

As she started for the door, Myrna wobbled a little. Cheyenne reached for her but didn't make contact. She knew her friend well enough to know she wouldn't want assistance.

"Myrna, why don't you stay and we'll have an early lunch together?"

Myrna reached for the door and turned to smile at Cheyenne. "I'm fine, honey. You'll see, by this afternoon I'll be right as rain. Right now I just need a little time to myself."

"Are you sure?"

Myrna patted Cheyenne's cheek with a cool hand. "I'm positive. It wasn't anything. I just decided to turn at the last minute, and I didn't pay attention to that truck coming from the other direction. Not only that, but knowing Larry, he was probably speeding and it served him right."

"If you're sure. But I could call someone."

"Not on your life do I want to call someone. I'm good."

Cheyenne stood at the window and watched Myrna drive away. The big car eased onto the road, a little slower, a little more cautious than usual. After a few minutes Cheyenne pulled the cell phone out of her pocket and searched a contact she hadn't called since that first time ten years ago.

This time she pushed the button and dialed. The phone rang several times, and an answering machine picked up. She started to end the call, but instead she left a message.

"Mom, it's me. I'm in Dawson, Oklahoma. This is my new number." She gave the number and ended the call. She could have given more information. She could have told them about Mark walking out on her, about the baby, about Reese. But all of the details of her life seemed too much for an answering machine. They only needed to know where she'd moved to and her number. If they wanted to call, they would.

After ending the call, she walked to the front window of her shop. There were no customers today. She didn't mind because she did need to rest. Her baby deserved a chance to make it to term. And if she slept, she might escape the worries that plagued her almost constantly.

The one thing she couldn't escape in her dreams happened to be her husband, Reese Cooper. If Myrna knew their secret, the rest of the family probably knew as well. So much for the plan to end things quietly.

Reese held the arm of the rehab specialist as Anna led him around the apartment, getting him acquainted with the way everything had been laid out. The furniture had been moved from the walking areas. The kitchen was set up for the easiest use.

He'd moved in Sunday evening, and he'd done a lot of creeping, trying not to fall over furniture or trip on obstacles he couldn't see.

"The kitchen is pretty basic, Reese. The problem you're going to have is the gas burners on the stove. Be very careful not to leave things too close."

"Like my arm."

"Well, a sleeve could be a danger." She laughed a little. "I've marked the knobs. Touch and get acquainted with where the dial turns and how the numbers line up."

"There's always the microwave."

"Very true but it will be good if you can use the stove. We'll work on basic cooking skills. Now let's walk to the bathroom. I have everything organized and labeled."

"Wouldn't want me to try shaving with bathroom tile cleaner," he teased, because teasing made it a lot easier to be guided from room to room, having his life explained to him this way.

"No, I wouldn't recommend that."

"Or using drain cleaner for mouthwash."

"Likewise, not a reasonable option." She touched his arm. "Lead the way to the bathroom. I'm right behind you."

With a curt nod, he unfolded his cane. It was kitchen to dining area, left turn through the living room. He walked twenty steps to the small hallway where there were two doors. The bedroom door was on the right. The bathroom door was on the left. He smiled as he walked through the door of the bathroom.

"I rock." He turned to where he knew Anna stood.

"You do." She touched his back and moved him to the cabinet. "You're doing great, Reese."

"Thanks."

"On a serious note, how are you sleeping?"

He sighed and reached to open the cabinet door. Braille was a foreign language at this point, but he was learning the raised bumps. And he knew how Anna had organized for him. There were three shelves. Toiletries were on the top; towels, washcloths and linens were in the middle; and cleaners were on the bottom.

"Reese, are you managing to sleep?"

"I'm okay, Anna. There are times when I have to get out of bed and do something to get it out of my mind, but it's getting better."

"You're still going to therapy?"

"Twice a month now."

"Good." She touched his arm. "I organized just the way I told you I would. Toiletries, towels, cleaners. The bottles are marked, but until you are positive, I have shampoo in square-shaped containers. Shaving cream is in the original can, of course and there are bars of soap."

"Gotcha."

"Have you seen any old friends? You know, life still has to be lived, Reese. Dates? Dinner with friends?"

"No." He laughed a little and didn't tell her he was a married man. "But I am working again."

"Working?"

"Around here. I'm a decent hand at feeding time. I can still put a horse on a long line." He touched the shelves of the cabinet. "I'm considering helping at a local youth camp."

"That's great to hear. Don't forget a social life."

"And now we should go make sure I know where my food is."

She laughed as he deflected. "Lead the way."

He did as she asked, leading her back to the kitchen, showing her his awesome coffee-making skills and how he could heat soup in the microwave. After another hour of "Reese Cooper, this is your life," Anna left.

Reese walked through the apartment by himself, touching the sofa, turning on the TV and then making his way to the kitchen. He stood in the center of the room, thinking about the way he remembered it—white cabinets, black granite countertops, stainless appliances. He poured himself a glass of water, drank it and then set the glass on the counter. He'd do himself a lot more good working than he would standing there wondering how to feel like a whole man, how to feel normal in his own skin.

He opened the door and walked down the narrow steps and out the garage into the hot July sun. When he reached the yard, he stood for a long moment getting his bearings. A lifetime of knowing which direction to turn and now he had to think about how to get to the stable. He pushed the hat back on his head and let it all settle. He had to do this on his own, not on someone's arm, not every day for the rest of his life.

He took a deep breath past the anger, the resentment. He faced the sun, letting the heat hit him full in the face. It was afternoon and the sun was west. The driveway was north, straight out from the garage. He crossed the driveway and found the fence. He heard a horse snort and then stomp, probably at flies or bees. In the distance a cow bellowed for her calf. He kept walking, occasionally touching his cane to the fence to make sure he still had it as a guide. When the cane hit wood, he knew he'd made it to the corral.

The barn was next. He slid his hand down the wall to the door, opened it and stepped inside. The aisle between the stalls was about fifteen feet wide. There were a dozen stalls, a tack room, a feed room and an office. Another aisle, midway down on the right, led to the indoor arena.

Reese stayed close to the stalls on the right, swinging the cane because when it hit open space, he knew to turn. He pulled back when something nipped at his leg. He reached down, and the scruffy pup licked his hand.

"Buddy, you'd better learn to either be a guide dog or stay back." He petted the dog on the neck, letting his fingers settle in thick fur. "You going with me?"

The dog barked a sharp woof and then stood on hind legs and rested his paws on Reese's leg.

Anna would be proud. He had a social life, a friend to hang out with. He had the six-month-old blue heeler Travis had named Skipper. He thought back to old episodes of *Lassie* and chuckled. If he had a Lassie, he wouldn't have to worry about falling over a cliff or down the well. Lassie would have blocked him from danger. He felt pretty sure this pup would lead him off a cliff given half a chance.

"Come on, then." He swung the cane back and forth, every now and then feeling a tug and knowing the pup had it in his mouth.

He got to the aisle that led to the arena. He could hear Jackson shouting out orders to run a bull through to the chute. For a minute Reese paused, listening to life going on. He stood there, unsure of a place he'd been in a thousand times in his life.

He had to trust the dark. He swallowed and kept walking. It would have been easy to stay in the house, to let his mom fix his meals, pick his clothes and lead him around by the arm. That wasn't who he was. He heard the clang of metal, and Travis shouted for someone to keep his hand in the rope. Reese smiled because this was his life and he didn't plan on letting go.

This ranch had always been his world. It would continue to be just that. The horses, the cattle, the bulls were what he knew, and he'd make it happen. If he kept working at it, he'd be able to live here and ranch the way he'd always planned—with adjustments.

He stopped when he hit the metal of the arena fence. If he turned left, there would be a narrow gap between the fence and the wall. He could follow that to the chutes and the pens where his brothers were working. Dust rolled around him. He could smell the cattle, hear them move and bump against the metal cattle panels.

This place hadn't changed. He had. Six months ago he'd been a lot younger, a lot more carefree. He stopped, holding tight to the cold metal pipe of the arena. In a flash he was back in Afghanistan, hearing the explosion, feeling the heat and the pain and then seeing nothing. He remembered his friends, the men in his care, yelling and some moaning in agony. He remained in the darkness, waiting for the light to return.

He'd been waiting for over two months now, but the light wouldn't return. The last images set in his mind were of the front of their vehicle blowing off and the driver disappearing in the blast.

The hymn "Amazing Grace" played through his mind. But the words switched: I could see, but now I'm blind. He continued to grip the metal pipe of the fence, holding on for a long moment to something real, something that wouldn't give, wouldn't change. He could walk along the outside of this corral, and in a few minutes he would be in familiar territory. He fought back the fear, the doubts that sometimes came at him. God hadn't dealt him a bad hand or let him down. A roadside bomb, not God, had taken his sight.

It was not that it was always easy to accept, but he was working on it. He had to or it would consume him. Each time the fear hit, he replaced it with what he knew was the truth and real. He slid his hand along the fence and kept walking until he touched the corner post. He smiled. Yeah, this was progress—one step at a time.

He turned and kept walking, now on the side of the arena where the chutes were located. A gate clanged again, and a bull bellowed loud. He paused, unsure.

"Reese," Jackson called out over the other noises, the clanging gates, the men talking and the bulls bellowing. "Come on over, we're trying to get Gage to hold on to a bull and not get tossed like a rag doll."

The cane hit something solid. Reese touched the metal of the chute and walked around it. Jackson said something about a new bull, and Travis let out a whoop and holler, probably running a bull back into the holding pen. Reese stopped next to Jackson and waited.

"Who's on now?"

Jackson grunted. "Jake Thompson, from down the road."

Jake was a teenager they'd known since he'd moved to the area a few years ago. "How's he doing?"

"Good. Gage had better start holding on or he's going to be off the pro tour and this kid will take his spot."

The buzzer rang. He jumped a little and waited. A minute later the gate opened.

"Gage needs your help or he isn't going to stay on a bull any time soon." Travis bumped against him. "Sit with me, and Jackson is going to put him on Hammer."

"I'm not sure how I can help him." He hit the gate with his cane and reached for the latch. He walked through and Travis followed, closing it behind them.

"He's going down in the well every time the bull turns into his hand."

Down in the well meant the bull would spin and the rider got pulled to the inside, into the vortex of the spin.

Reese sighed and remembered back to when he'd ridden bulls and then to the last few years when he'd been out of the sport but coaching his younger brothers. He would sit for hours and watch, give them tips, help them when they couldn't seem to keep their seat.

He'd been a decent coach. They'd brought their friends. They'd brought guys home from the circuit who had mentally pushed themselves from the game and couldn't stay on a bull for nothing.

"I can't help him, Trav."

"Yeah, you can. Gage, get back in here!" he shouted out to their younger brother.

"Travis," Jackson's voice growled from not too far away. It was a warning for Travis not to push.

"I'll give details of what Gage is doing wrong, and Reese can tell him what he needs to do to fix the problem. Come on, guys. If Gage doesn't do something he's going to get hurt, and Reese is the one who can help."

"You're probably right about that," Gage muttered as he walked past them. "I'm just about sick of this whole mess."

"You're sick of everything." Jackson's voice grew louder. "Reese, don't let Travis push you."

"I'm not." He leaned against the fence. "Has anyone seen Dad?"

"Gran had a near miss in town. Larry called and said he almost T-boned her in the middle of the intersection by the Mad Cow." Jackson answered, grunting as he spoke, which meant he was getting the bull rope on Hammer.

"Granny?" Reese couldn't believe it. Their grandmother had to be the brightest, most with-it woman he knew. "What's gotten into her?"

"I don't know, but Larry said she was babbling about her granddaughter." Jackson moved past him, moving him to the side a little. "Won't be long before the whole town knows. And then they're going to wonder why she's living in the barbershop and you're out here."

"I'll figure something out." Reese moved as Gage stepped in close to climb on the bull. "Where are you, Travis? Get over here so you can give me the play-by-play. And what do I get for doing this?"

"A trip to town for you to get a haircut. You obviously don't know how bad you look." Jackson moved next to him again, climbing on the side of the chute where the bull clanked against the metal gates and bellowed low as Gage settled on his back.

"Really, you think I can't see how bad I look?" Jackson groaned. "Sorry."

"No, really, it's okay. What do you think I should do about it?" He rolled his shoulders and started thinking about a place to sit down. A hand touched his arm.

"We can sit down over here." Travis moved him away from the chute, around the corner to the risers where spectators sat when they held events.

"Married life is making you soft, Trav." Reese eased down and stretched his legs out in front of him. Man, it did feel good to sit down.

"You should try it." Travis laughed. "Oh, wait. You have. Kind of."

"Funny."

"I have more bad news."

"What's that?"

"Heather made you an appointment to get your hair cut. Jackson is hinting because he didn't want to be the one to tell you that the females in this family can't mind their own business."

"Nice, real nice. And is it your job to drive me to get this haircut?"

"Yeah, we've got an hour before the appointment."

"Great."

"Jackson is opening the gate." Travis leaned close.

Reese waited. The gate creaked as it opened, and then the bull snorted and hooves pounded.

"Tell me." Reese leaned forward, listening.

"Coming out of the gate he's leaning hard left. It's every time, like he's waiting for something that doesn't happen. And then he tries to correct. He can't get his free arm up."

Hooves pounded. The bull snorted. Jackson yelled for Gage to get off his seat and ride the bull. He needed to make corrections, meaning get back in the center of the bull's back. Reese could almost visualize his brother bouncing farther and farther off the back end of the bull and not moving himself forward into position after each jump of the animal.

"What's he doing with his free arm?"

"Straight back, behind him. Every time the bull goes forward, Gage gets back on his pockets and flings around like a rag doll."

Reese shrugged. "You know as well as I do that he's not using his arm to correct the moves. Instead it's pulling him back."

"Gotcha." Travis moved again, shifting and leaning forward. "He's off."

"Six seconds?"

No answer.

"Are you nodding?" he asked his brother.

"Sorry." Travis leaned back. "Yeah, six seconds. I'll go tell him what you said and then we'll head to town for that haircut."

"He needs to ride again, and Jackson needs to run the camera and get a video of it. Tell him to keep his chin tucked and his elbow bent. Maybe that'll keep him from getting flung backward. It's mental. He's got something on his mind or he's afraid of getting hurt."

"Got it. Hey, did Adam MacKenzie call you about Camp Hope?"

"Yeah, I've talked to him. I'm not sure if I

can do that. I think I'd be more trouble than I'm worth."

"Way to sell yourself short, brother." Travis let out a breath that Reese imagined was followed by a disappointed shake of his head. "I'll be back."

Reese stood, and Travis walked away leaving him to navigate on his own. The arena was in front of him, to the right the chutes. He turned to the right, taking careful steps between the arena and the bleachers. He could hear Travis giving Gage the tips that might or might not help him stay on a bull. Reese started to say something about focus, but he couldn't force Gage to get his mind on the sport. Something else had to be going on for Gage to be taking this many spills.

He'd love to stay and think about Gage's problems, but he had enough going on in his own life to keep him busy. He didn't have to guess where Travis would take him for the haircut. He knew how Heather's mind worked.

Chapter Seven

"Little baby, you have to stay in there for a few more weeks."

Cheyenne stretched in the little chair that Myrna had given her, resting her hand on her belly as she glanced at the clock. The contractions weren't regular, and they were light. She breathed a sigh of relief. At this point, talking to her unborn child and to herself seemed like more of a problem than the contractions.

From her chair she could see the front of the shop, and through the windows she could see the street. There hadn't been much traffic today, but she'd had a few customers. She watched as a truck pulled to a stop parallel to the curb. The big red Ford blocked her view of the street. The passenger side door opened, and Reese stepped out, easing to the ground and then holding the door for a long moment. She could see him getting his bearings. Before Travis reached his side, Reese had a smile in place.

Her heart squeezed a little, watching as the two men walked across the sidewalk to her door. She'd forgotten the appointment Heather Cooper made for Reese. She jumped up and slipped her feet into the shoes she'd bought the previous day—extra wide for swollen feet.

This is what her life had been reduced to. She couldn't eat chips because her fingers would puff up so big that she couldn't bend them. She had to wear wide shoes because being on her feet caused them to swell like water balloons. And every night when she tried to go to sleep, heartburn hit with a vengeance.

None of it seemed to be really important when she thought about what Reese Cooper faced each day. Somehow he managed to smile. He managed to be strong. She tried to stop the flow of thoughts that included how he made her feel, because she didn't quite know what she felt. It seemed like dangerous ground, to feel something.

The two men were still outside. Travis leaned close. Reese said something. They laughed and then Reese shook his head. She tried not to be the hormonal female who thought they were talking about her. Instead she swept the floor and made sure she had shampoo and a towel at the sink.

The door to the shop opened. She set the shampoo bottle on the edge of the sink and turned, pasting on a welcoming smile that faltered a little. Reese folded his white cane and took off the sunglasses he often wore. He eased the sunglasses into the pocket of his button-up shirt and then slid the cane into the pocket of faded jeans.

"I'm assuming you're here." He grinned, flashing white teeth in a suntanned face.

"I'm here."

"I knew that. You're the noisiest quiet person I've ever met."

"I'm not."

He took a few steps forward and she waited.

"You are. You move a lot. And sigh."

"It's your imagination."

He smiled again and this time leaned a little. "And you smell like lavender."

"It's shower gel." Heat crawled into her cheeks. "I mean..."

She had no idea what she meant. She rarely did with Reese around. She especially didn't know how to handle this Reese, the one who flirted and teased. She shifted her attention to Travis, who had taken a step back.

"So I guess the two of you are good if I leave for a while?" Travis grinned and winked at Cheyenne. And she ignored him, because he thought he knew something about them, and he didn't.

"I think we're good." Reese slid his hand up to the bend of her arm and held tight. "Where are you going?"

Travis had already made it to the front door. He stopped to answer. "I have to run to the feed store and of course Vera's, for pie. I'll be back in an hour."

"That should be good." She watched Travis walk out the door and cross to his truck. She looked at Reese again. "Do you think we could take off the hat?"

He smiled and removed the bent-up black cowboy hat. "No problem."

She took it from him and set it on the counter. "You need to shave."

"Yeah, so I've been told. To be honest, it isn't that easy."

"I can do it for you while you're here."

"I might just let you."

She led him to the back of the shop, to a chair in front of the sink. She guided him into the seat and he eased down, staring straight ahead. She couldn't look at him. She couldn't think about his life, what he was thinking or what he wanted. Instead she gathered what she would need: the plastic cape, towel, shampoo. She found a razor and shaving cream.

"What are you doing?" He turned in her direction.

"Getting ready. Lean forward a little."

"Could you do me a favor?"

She stopped and looked down, at hazel eyes staring up at her, not seeing her. "I can."

"I'd feel a lot less alone in the dark if you'd tell me step by step what you're doing."

"I'm so sorry, I didn't think…"

He smiled and offered an easy wink. "We're all learning."

"Okay." She smoothed the towel and leaned the chair. "Tilt your head forward so I can wrap this towel around your neck."

He leaned and she draped the towel, but she hesitated. A jagged scar marred the skin on the back of his neck. She touched it, and he turned toward her hand.

"Shrapnel," he explained.

"I see." Her throat constricted, and she took a deep breath, blinking away the moisture blurring her vision. "Lean back."

She turned on the water, got it warm, and he put his head back. Okay, she could do this. She could make him nothing to her, just a person who needed a haircut.

"You're not going to hurt me." His head rested on the padded edge of the sink, and she nodded as she squirted shampoo in her hand. "Cheyenne?"

"I know I won't. I'm getting the water the right temperature."

She poured a little shampoo in her hand and hesitated before massaging it through his hair. He closed his eyes, a hint of a smile curving his lips. He whispered that she had an amazing touch.

She couldn't comment.

"Rinsing. Close your eyes," she whispered moments later.

He nodded a barely perceptible nod with his head still resting on the edge of the sink. After the water ran clear, she leaned him forward and rubbed the towel through his hair. Sandy brown, it curled at the collar of his shirt.

"Okay, let's move to the barber chair." The antique had been in the shop and no way would she get rid of it. It was part of Dawson history. Some said a former president, long before he'd been president, had once had a haircut in that chair. The residents spoke fondly of his fishing trip in the area and what a gentleman he'd been.

Reese pushed himself up from the chair, and she took his hand. "Watch for that footrest. It'll get you."

"Got it." He stepped over the metal bar in question

"Over here. Have a seat and I'll get my clippers."

"I don't want to have my head shaved, just trimmed."

"I'm not going to shave your head." She laughed a little, and it sounded tight and uneasy. "Relax."

"Can you?"

"What?"

"Relax. I can feel your hands tremble every time you touch me. Are you worried?"

"Of course not."

"Think how I feel. You could dye my hair pink, and I'd never know."

"Someone would tell you."

He laughed at that. "Would they?"

"Maybe after a day or two."

He sat down in the old pump-up barber seat. The hydraulics still worked, and the foot pedal raised him to a height that made it easy for her to reach. She ran a comb through his still-damp hair, and then she lifted her scissors and snipped the first inch of hair. He closed his eyes and remained quiet while she cut.

"It already feels better," he whispered as she put her scissors away and reached for the clippers to trim the back.

"I'm sure it does. Now hold still. I'm going to clean it up along the neck with clippers."

She turned on the clippers and finished the job. When she looked at him with his hair cut, she remembered back to that day in Vegas. He'd been tall and straight but relaxed. He'd held her arm as he'd guided her back into the restaurant, to a corner booth. She'd been a mess, a sobbing mess nearly ready to collapse. She'd bumped into him as she'd hurried out of the restaurant.

"All done?" His question brought her back to the present.

She nodded and then she answered. "Let me get shaving cream, and we'll take off a few layers of facial hair."

"It isn't that bad. I shaved a few days ago."

She smiled and touched his cheek, brushing her palm across the stubble. "It's pretty bad."

"Go for it, then."

She walked away, returning a moment later with shaving cream and a razor. "Hold still."

"Or you'll cut my neck?"

"I wouldn't do it on purpose."

He laughed, and it was a soft, throaty chuckle. "Well, that's good to know."

She wet a towel with warm water and draped it over his face for a moment. When she moved it, he turned to face her. She ignored questions she saw in his expression. With hands that trembled, she squirted shaving cream into her palm and then brushed it across his face. He closed his eyes and exhaled as she ran the razor across his cheeks the first time. She held his jaw with the tips of her fingers on her left hand and shaved him with her right—a swipe with the razor and then rinse.

Her hands stopped trembling. His eyes remained closed. Her heart took up trembling where her hands left off. And finally she finished, wiping away the last traces of shaving cream.

"All done."

"Thank you." He pushed himself up from the chair and then turned, reaching for her, finding her arm. "Come here."

Stop, the little voice in her head warned. Instead she flicked away the voice of reason and stepped close because her heart cried for him, for someone to hold, to hold her back. She'd been alone for so long. She'd been afraid for herself, for him.

His last letter to her had warned that he might be needing some extra prayers as he went into a dangerous situation. She'd never been so afraid in her life. But now, looking back, by the time she got that letter, he'd probably already been injured.

"I'm here," she whispered, eyes closed, inhaling the scent of him as he moved to draw her closer.

He reached, touching her face, her cheek. He traced his fingers along her jaw to her lips and then he leaned and she couldn't breathe, couldn't stop the inevitable from happening. His lips touched hers, and she moved farther into his arms.

He kissed her slow and easy and then he paused in his exploration of her lips, her cheek, the spot close to her ear. He whispered that she tasted like cinnamon. He kissed her again, taking his time, his fingers resting lightly on her cheek.

"You're beautiful." His freshly shaved cheek brushed hers.

She couldn't respond. She leaned, resting her forehead on his shoulder. He wrapped strong arms around her and held her close to him.

"Reese, we shouldn't do this."

He released a shaky breath that she felt as he held her. "I'm not sorry."

"I'm…" She didn't know what to say. What did she tell him about her feelings and her doubts about the future? How did she explain that her whole life she'd felt rejected, like the person easiest to part with. And the marriage certificate meant nothing, nothing more than a good deed. When it was over, they would part ways and she'd be the forgotten woman he'd once married.

"Cheyenne. I'm sorry." He reached, touching her cheek and brushing at the tears she couldn't stop.

For what? The kiss? Marrying her? Or for not loving her? And she really didn't expect him to. This had all turned into a big mess, and she needed to do something to fix it. If she hadn't come here…

"You don't need to be sorry." She blinked away the last of her tears and managed to smile. "This is going to pass, and we'll get back to normal."

"Will we?" He said it with a soft voice that brushed against her heart.

"I don't know. Maybe not. The whole town is going to know you married a pregnant showgirl from Vegas." She laughed a little through her tears. "That would be a great line on the wedding announcement. Mr. and Mrs. Tim Cooper announce the marriage of their son, Reese, to a dancer from Vegas."

He didn't smile. "I'm not ashamed of you, and my parents aren't ashamed of you if that's what you think."

It was, but she didn't comment.

Reese moved to a chair and sat down. He pulled her with him, his hand still holding hers tight. "I want you to move out to the ranch."

"Move out to the ranch? With you?"

"We have an apartment in the stable. I know that sounds kind of bleak, but it's actually pretty nice. It was a bunkhouse at one time, and Travis remodeled it."

"Why would I move out there?"

"Because we have plenty of room, and it's a lot better than living in the storeroom of a barbershop. And because if you don't, people are really going to talk."

"What does that mean?"

"When word spreads that we're married, they're going to wonder why you're living here."

She reached for the broom and started to clean up. "You're worried about what people will think."

"That isn't what I mean." But the look on his face, the frown, convinced her otherwise.

She glanced to the front of the shop when a shadow flashed across the room. A truck parked. His brother got out, stood on the sidewalk a minute talking on the phone and then walked up to the front door.

"Travis is here. You should go."

"We need to finish this discussion."

She knew it wasn't fair to walk away, but she needed space. She needed to breathe deep and not get caught up in wishing her temporary marriage could be something more.

From the books, she'd learned that pregnancy made a woman more emotional. They had strange cravings. They wanted to nest and make a place for their unborn child. She had to separate emotions from this relationship because wanting him in her life had a lot to do with the need for stability. She was sure of it. She didn't crave eggs, pickles or ice cream. She craved stability and love. And she knew better than to transfer that craving to the man standing in the center of her salon.

She turned when she reached her tiny room. "Let's just get the annulment. I don't need the protection of your last name. It was sweet, what you did, but it's time to bring this to an end. No one in town will ever know that we were married."

"Cheyenne, running away from me isn't fair."

"No, it isn't, but it's all I've got." She glanced to the front of the store and breathed a sigh of relief when Travis opened the door. "Travis is coming in."

"Great."

The door opened, the bell chimed and Travis smiled a big cowboy smile that quickly faded when he looked from one of them to the other.

"All finished?" Travis asked as he walked up to Reese. He grabbed the black hat from the counter and dropped it on his brother's head. "You look pretty."

"Yep, all finished and he's ready to go home," she answered.

Reese turned, not smiling. "I can answer for myself. And I'll see you at six."

"Six?"

"Dinner at the ranch."

She didn't answer. Reese left with his brother, and Cheyenne sank into one of the chairs at the front of the store, breathing through another contraction. In the middle of it all, her phone rang. The Kansas number flashed across the caller ID. Fear tangled with dread and hope. She answered it, a little breathless, and waited for the person on the other end.

"Hello?"

"Mom?" Cheyenne whispered, unsure.

"It's me. I got your message. Cheyenne, we've been praying you'd call us. We've—" her mother cried "—I'm so glad you're safe."

"I'm safe." She watched the truck out front pull away, and then she smiled and continued the conversation with her mother. And it didn't hurt as bad as she always thought it would.

Travis didn't say much on the way home. Not until they were going up the drive did he finally turn the radio off and clear his throat.

"What did you do to her?"

Reese shrugged and nearly told his brother it wasn't any of his business. But Travis had a way of getting things from a person that they never planned on sharing. If he had to, Reese knew his brother would drive this truck until it ran out of gas.

"Not that it is any of your business, but she believes I'm worried about what people will say when they hear that I married a Vegas showgirl."

In answer, Travis laughed. "I'd say that most of them will congratulate you."

"Talk like that again and you'll find out that I can still take you, Travis."

"Calm down. I'm just saying people around here aren't going to be sorry for you. She's a pretty girl and sweet. Everyone in town seems to like her."

"She thinks they'll look down on her. Or that I'll be embarrassed."

"Guess you'll have to show her she's wrong."

Reese rubbed the back of his neck and leaned back in the seat. "I'm just so stinking tired, Travis. I'm tired of trying to figure out which foot to put first, which direction to go."

"I guess you know what Mom would say."

"Pray." Reese sighed. "Yeah, sometimes it's not easy, is it? It's like knowing how to swim but you get panicked and you can't make it out of three feet of water."

Travis cleared his throat, downshifted and eased up the driveway. "I'll be praying for you."

"I know you will." Reese nodded and then switched topics. "Drop me off at the barn."

"Need anything before I head home to Elizabeth?"

"No, I'm good."

The truck stopped. "Here you go. Need…"

Reese turned and shook his head. "I can get it from here."

"I know."

Reese opened the door and stepped out of the truck. He could get there from here. He unfolded the cane and walked forward, stopping when the cane hit a solid obstacle. He moved a few feet to the right, found the corral fence and went back to the left, running his hand down the side of the barn until he got to the door.

As he walked through the barn, he thought back to what he would have done a year ago if he'd been this overwhelmed, this tied up in knots. He moved to the side of the aisle and touched a stall door. A year ago he would have saddled his horse and went for a ride. That's what he'd been doing his whole life.

"What's stopping me?" Two stalls away from the front entrance, he reached and a big head pushed at his hand. "Charlie, I've missed you."

He felt along the wall and found a lead rope. Easing the door open, he stepped inside and grabbed Charlie by the halter. He snapped the lead in place and led the big horse out of the stall.

"What are you going to do now?" The voice came from behind him.

He stopped and Charlie stopped next to him. "Me and Charlie are going for a ride."

"You can't—" Gage cleared his throat. "I meant to say, let me get his saddle."

"I'd appreciate that." He hadn't given it a thought, how he'd manage to throw a saddle on the back of a sixteen-hand quarter horse.

He led Charlie down the aisle to the tack room. "Hey, get me a brush, too."

A brush pressed into his hands—no words. Reese cross-tied the horse in the center of the aisle. Charlie tried to push at him, but the horse's head wouldn't turn that far.

"What's up with you lately?" He ran the brush down Charlie's muscled-up neck and then across his back. Charlie twitched, but he didn't move. He brushed the horse out and then tossed the brush toward the tack room.

Gage nudged him to the side. "Let me get him saddled for you. If you insist on breaking your neck, the least I can do is save your back."

"Thanks." Reese patted the horse's neck and then ran a hand along his face. He heard the creak of leather as Gage slid the saddle in place. "Got the bridle?"

"In a sec."

"Gage, I'm a pretty good listener."

"I know you are." Gage grunted, probably pulling the girth strap.

"Girl problems?"

"Nope."

"Fear?"

"Nope."

Reese slid a hand down his horse's neck, touched the saddle, found the saddle horn and gave it a good yank. It stayed put.

"Anything I can do to help?" He gave it one more shot, and then he knew to leave it be.

"Thanks, but no."

"Let me know…"

"I will." Gage pushed a bridle into his hand. "So you're putting the bridle on him?"

"Yep." He had the bit in his left hand and the headstall in his right. Charlie didn't fight him, never had. He'd taken the bit like a pro from the beginning.

"He's ready to go."

"I'm just going to ride in the arena."

"Smart thinking." Gage touched his elbow. "Let's go."

"You can go back to doing whatever you were doing." Reese led the horse through the gate and into the arena.

"Right, and if Mom happens to walk out here, I'm in big, big trouble. I'll leave trouble up to you. It's nice having a break and letting *you* be the brother pulling the stunt of a lifetime."

"Yeah, well, I'm not a kid and I guess it isn't really a stunt."

Gage laughed. "You married someone you'd known for a couple of hours. That pretty much gets the trophy for stunts pulled."

"Yeah, true that." He pulled the reins back and found the stirrup. "Here we go."

"Reese, be careful." Gage's voice got a little quieter. "Seriously, this is a little crazy."

"I'm good."

"I know."

Reese put his left foot in the stirrup and found that swinging his right leg over wasn't as easy as it used to be. But he managed. Holding the saddle horn, he pushed past the pain that sliced through his back and he settled into the seat. And it felt like coming home. He had both feet in the stirrups, the reins easy in his hand and Charlie whinnied a soft "welcome back."

He loosened up on the reins, and the gelding broke into an easy walk. It took Reese a minute to get his balance, to figure out his seat and how to ride without sight. He had to trust Charlie—completely. He'd always trusted the big gelding, but this went beyond that old trust that had relied on his own senses, most of all his eyesight.

With complete trust, he let out a pent-up breath and relaxed a little as Charlie rounded the arena without hesitation. With complete faith, he held the reins loose, gave Charlie the okay and the horse broke into an easy trot. He was completely humbled.

This was the place in his life where he accepted what he couldn't change. But he had faith to stand on something stronger, more reliable than himself. He had a God who had never left him, never forsaken him. *I was blind, but now I see. Amazing Grace.*

He pulled back on the reins and eased Charlie back to a walk. They circled the arena a few times, and then he gave the horse his head and Charlie broke into an easy lope. He steadied himself, waiting for the turns as the horse rounded the arena. Finally he pulled back and Charlie slowed to a stop. He rested the reins on the horse's neck, turning him to the right. But then he had to get his bearings. He'd been around the arena several times. The gate would be in the back corner.

"Gage?"

"Here. You're heading in the right direction."

Reese eased the gelding forward, following his brother's voice.

"You can take the cowboy out of the saddle..."

Gage laughed. "I'm pretty sure there's no saying for that."

"Yeah, probably not, but it feels pretty good to be on old Charlie."

"I have to bring in some steers tomorrow for vaccinations. You want to come with me?"

Reese tightened his legs. Charlie stopped, shifting beneath him, the saddle giving a little heave as the horse released a breath. "If it's before or after physical therapy I'm in."

"You're good with this?"

"As long as you realize you're going to have to give me some cues."

"I can do that, Reese." And then a short pause. "It's about time for supper."

"Thanks." Reese eased his right foot from the stirrup, swung it over the saddle and dropped to the ground. "Thanks, Charlie, old guy."

The horse pushed against his arm. Reese rubbed the sleek neck and then slipped the reins over his head to lead him back to the stable. He'd invited Cheyenne for supper with the family. As crazy as it seemed, he wanted her on the ranch. At least here she'd be taken care of. If something happened, she'd have people with her.

He figured he had other reasons for wanting

her close, but they were his and pretty selfish, like the one where he didn't want to let her go.

And she seemed pretty determined to end this marriage as soon as possible.

Chapter Eight

Cheyenne pulled up to the big Georgian-style home and sat in her old car. A moment of déjà vu hit. Just over a couple of weeks ago she'd sat in her car staring up at that house, afraid to face the man she'd married, worried about his health. Today she had fewer questions about her future but more questions about the man she'd married.

They seemed to be in a careful game of cat and mouse, moving close, backing away. But she knew, and she thought Reese knew it, too, that they couldn't be a real couple. They weren't a couple. Period. This family wasn't hers. She didn't belong to any of them—not even to Reese.

She actually had a family. She thought through the conversation with her mother. They hadn't really said much that counted, hadn't admitted to the pain they'd caused each other, but they'd talked. It had been easy talk about life, about being pregnant, about her sister's marriage. They had talked like it hadn't been ten years.

A dog barked. She looked and saw the dog. She saw Reese. He walked next to a younger man who looked a lot like him. And if she didn't know about his accident, she wouldn't have guessed that he couldn't see. The two men walked side by side and both wore jeans, boots and button-up shirts. Reese wore his black cowboy hat. The other, younger version of Reese wore a white hat. They walked with matching, casual strolls, an easy gait, loose-limbed and confident.

The only thing that gave Reese away was the white cane he swung in front of him, the occasional pause in his step as he adjusted. She stepped out of her car. The dog ran to greet her, barking sharply and then wagging its stubby tail and licking the palm of her hand when she reached to pet him.

"Cheyenne?" Reese called out, turning in her direction.

"Yes." She'd come for dinner. She didn't need to tell him. He had invited her. Actually, it had been more of an order than an invitation.

His brother said something, touched Reese's arm and then walked across the driveway to get in a big four-wheel drive truck. She watched him back out and leave. Reese walked toward her.

"You're here." He stopped just a few feet away.

"I'm here." She looked away from him, from the handsome cowboy whom she'd married. She hadn't thought about attraction between them. She hadn't planned on caring about him.

The letters... She shouldn't have written the letters. It had felt like courting. The letters had created this strange, tenuous bond between them. Without those letters they would have remained strangers.

She knew that he wanted a home on his fifty acres of Cooper land. He wanted cattle. He had a degree in counseling. He loved his family.

He had connections, roots.

She was a tiny boat adrift on a big, open ocean. But at least now she had an anchor. She hadn't had an anchor in years. She closed her eyes and prayed that God would help her do the right thing, to not hold on to Reese because it made her life more secure to have him close.

"You're still here, right?" Reese's question pulled her back and she realized that she'd drifted.

"I'm here."

"You're nervous?"

"A little." She glanced from Reese to the

Cooper home. "I'm a stranger, and you're going to take me in there and introduce me as your wife. Right? And they're all going to look at me like I'm using you. Or worse."

"They know better." He pulled off his sunglasses. "Do you want to hide behind these?"

She looked into hazel eyes and fought the urge to reach up and touch his face. "No. Is that what you do?"

He smiled and put them back on. "No. Well, maybe sometimes. There are a few reasons I wear them. I can't see the sun, so I don't know to look away. Sunburned eyes is not something I enjoy. It also makes people feel more comfortable if I'm not staring without realizing I'm staring. And in a crowded room it makes people notice that I can't see—that and the cane—and they're more considerate."

"I understand."

"Maybe you could join me for rehab. They say it's helpful for family to understand."

"Reese, I'm not really family."

"No, I guess not. I just thought…"

"We should go inside."

"And not discuss this." He shot her an easy grin and started forward, the white cane swinging easily from side to side in front of him. It hit the first step and he stopped, found the rail and started up. "You're with me, right?"

"Right here."

He nodded and continued up. When they reached the porch, the door opened. Heather stepped out, a welcoming smile reaching out to Cheyenne as she gestured for them to enter the foyer.

"Cheyenne, I'm glad you made it."

"Thank you." Cheyenne didn't know what else to say to a family dinner with the Coopers on a Tuesday evening. She could smell the grill.

"Everyone else is out back on the patio. Did you bring a swimsuit?"

"No." She looked down at her belly, and Heather closed her eyes briefly.

"I'm so sorry. I didn't think." Heather shook her head and her gaze remained on Cheyenne's belly. "Is he kicking like crazy?"

"Right now?" Cheyenne ran her hand over her belly. "Yes. See him moving?"

Reese's hand touched her arm. Cheyenne turned, facing him and facing a tumult of emotions that swept through her, making it hard to breathe.

"I'm going to go tell the family that you're here." Heather smiled quickly and hurried away. "Don't be too long or someone else will come looking for you. And, Reese, you smell like a horse."

"Thanks." He spoke with a husky, heavy voice.

"Reese?" Why were they still standing in the foyer? Why did it hurt to breathe? Why did he do this to her when she told herself she wouldn't let it happen, this feeling of being connected to him.

"I want to know what the baby is doing." He shook his head and laughed just a little. "I feel like I'm missing out on something really important. And I know that doesn't make sense."

"I know." She knew that it didn't make sense. She knew that it felt as if he was missing out. Or maybe she was the one missing out on him being involved with this baby. She didn't really know. She reached for his hand, and as her little guy did a somersault in her belly she placed Reese's hand, calloused and strong, on her shirt.

He was her husband. She closed her eyes as he stepped close but not before she saw his smile. He laughed a little and shook his head in wonder.

"Amazing." He moved his hand to her arm, up to her shoulder and then to her face. His fingers touched her cheek, her chin, and then they stroked her jaw, down to her neck. He leaned in close, not smelling like a horse but like a man who had been outdoors. He smelled good and clean. He kissed her cheek and then he held her close.

"Thank you."

She nodded because she couldn't answer.

"We should go." He pulled back, but he held out his hand and she took it.

They walked through the house to the kitchen. Bright sunlight came through the big windows and the French door that led to the patio. Through the glass she could see the family gathered around the pool. There were several patio tables and a covered outdoor kitchen.

One of the men on the patio saw them coming and opened the door. Cheyenne searched her memory but couldn't recall him. He had dark hair and hazel eyes that matched Reese's strong features. Cut from stone, she thought. He was strong and serious.

"Reese, do you want your burger well-done?" the man asked.

"Blake, this is Cheyenne. And you do know how to get right to the point."

"Sorry." Blake smiled at her and held out a strong hand. "Blake Cooper. Older brother."

"Nice to meet you." And it was nerve-racking.

"Come on out. We're taking burgers off the

grill. Do you like cheese?" He motioned them onto the patio.

"I do. Thanks." She started to move, but the world blurred a little. She blinked quick and managed to smile at Blake Cooper. He gave her a funny look and walked away.

"You okay?" Reese grunted a little. "Because you sure have a grip."

She breathed deep and closed her eyes. "I'm good."

"Nervous?"

"A little. You have a huge family."

"They bite." He held on to her hand. "But don't worry, I'll protect you."

"Thanks. I think."

Reese held her back. "Cheyenne, I wish you would think about moving to the ranch. With preeclampsia, I think it's important for you to be where we can help you."

"Do you know what preeclampsia is?"

He laughed and shook his head. "I'm pretty sure I don't."

"I'm fine, Reese." She looked past him to the family lining up at the counter near the grill.

"I know you are, but I'll rest easier if you're here. You can drive my truck. Your car has a serious death knock."

"'Death knock'? What does that mean?"

"The engine is about to go." He looped his arm through hers. "After dinner I'll show you the stable apartment. Don't let the word *stable* put you off. When you see what Travis did with the old bunkhouse, you'll be impressed."

"I'll think about it."

"Good. And in return, I'll let you lead me over to the grill where I will show you how amazing I am at fixing my own plate."

She smiled and nodded her head because she couldn't do more. Her head ached and her feet were swollen. As much as she wanted to fight Reese on moving to the ranch, she couldn't because she no longer wanted to be alone.

She wanted to be with people. She wanted to be around Reese.

Reese waited until most of the family had left before he asked Cheyenne to walk with him. He wanted to show her the stable apartment. But he also wanted a few minutes alone with her. It had something to do with summer, tree frogs and warm air. In the distance he heard a coyote howl. Next to him Cheyenne shivered.

"They won't bother us," he assured her as they walked across the yard.

"I know. It's the melancholy sound."

"Yeah, I know." He continued walking, and

he nodded in the general direction of the garage. "I live in the guesthouse over the garage. It isn't quite as amazing as the bunkhouse."

"I find that hard to believe. I haven't seen anything on this ranch that isn't amazing."

"Including me?" he teased.

"You're definitely amazing." Her tone caught him by surprise. Cheyenne was flirting. He smiled and switched his cane to his left hand so he could slide his right arm around her waist. The gesture felt comfortable, as if he'd always known her, always had her in his life.

When they reached the barn, he opened the door and motioned her inside. "After you."

"You're getting very good at this." She touched his hand and drew him back to her side.

"Yeah, it's getting easier." He moved to the left side of the stable. "The apartment is the last door on the end. It even has a small fenced-in yard and a patio."

"Seriously?"

"For real." He swung his cane until it hit solid wall, not the boards of the stalls. "Here we go."

He reached and found the door handle. Once they were inside, he led her to the kitchen. "Granite countertops, new appliances. And the paintings on the walls are compliments of my very artistic brother."

"Amazing. Can we turn on lights?" She stepped away from him and flipped a switch.

He laughed. "Yeah, sure, if you insist on not being in the dark."

"I never thought about it, Reese. You don't turn on lights."

"No need." He opened the freezer and felt inside. "Still food in here. At first I turned on lights. Out of habit, I guess."

"I'm sure."

He led her from the kitchen, through the living room and the room that was once an art studio, then to the bedroom.

"What do you think?" He walked back to the living room and sat down. Cheyenne didn't join him. He listened as she walked around from room to room. Occasionally she paused.

"It's amazing. You were right. But I don't know if I can do this."

"No strings, Cheyenne. It's a place to live. It's more comfortable than a storeroom in an old barbershop."

"I know. I guess it's too late to care what people think of me."

"What do they think?"

"I don't know. I'm sure there are people who think I'm using you." She sat down on the trunk that served as a coffee table, and her hands touched his. "I feel like I'm using you. Like I've used you. That isn't a good feeling. Not when I'm trying so hard to be strong and make a good life for myself."

He grasped her hand. "I think we help each other."

"But you have family and friends all around you."

"You're right. They all want to help. But I need independence. I need a ride to Tulsa tomorrow. I have a perfectly good truck in the garage that I can't drive. And you have a car that needs to be parked."

"You're suggesting this is a way to help each other." She leaned and kissed his cheek. "Very sweet way to make me feel like I'm not using you."

"Did it work?" He cleared his throat and thought about that kiss on the cheek. Sometimes the most innocent gesture could rattle a guy.

"Yeah, I think it did."

"Good, but I'm serious about needing your help." He sat back and she moved to the couch but not close enough to touch. He wanted to tell her how much he needed her at the ranch. She brought a sense of normalcy his world had been missing.

Before he could tell her, a shrill whinny interrupted. She let go of his hand. "What was that?"

He stood. "I'm not sure. Someone is pretty upset."

Cheyenne followed him out the door and into the stable. The horse whinnied again. He followed the sound to a stall at the far end—not Charlie but the horse next to him. Reese turned, looking for Cheyenne.

"Are you here?"

"I'm right behind you." She leaned in close. "Oh, Reese."

"What's going on?" He unlatched the stall door, but he didn't plan on going in until he had a little more information.

"I think she's having a baby."

"And you think this why?" He stepped a foot into the stall and found the mare's halter. "Cheyenne, I need information. You have to be my eyes."

"There are hooves. She's shaking."

"Good. Okay." He ran a hand down the horse's neck and reached into his pocket for his phone. "Call Jackson. If he doesn't answer, call Travis. Go down the list until someone answers."

She took the phone, and he moved down the mare's side. He could hear Cheyenne muttering as she used his phone. And then he heard her talking to someone.

Without sight, he had to think back to other situations, other mares. Usually horses delivered without a lot of complications. They might wait for hours until no one was around to watch. The main complication was the occasional thick sack that a foal had trouble breaking loose from. They'd lost an Arab foal that way once. The little filly couldn't break from the sack and she'd suffocated.

He knew in seconds that this was a different problem. He ran his hand down the mare's rump and examined her. This baby was coming out with one hoof lodged in the birth canal. So much for a relaxing night on the ranch. The mare sidestepped around. He moved when she moved and wished like crazy that he could see.

But his hands knew what to do. He'd done this before—not often, but a few times.

"You're going to deliver this baby?" Cheyenne gasped a little and leaned in close.

"Could you hand me a lead rope? There should be one hanging next to the stall door. Who'd you get hold of?"

"Jesse."

He laughed. "Okay, that works."

"I have the lead rope." Her voice trembled a little.

"Cheyenne, you don't have to be afraid. Just clip that on the bottom of her halter, the metal ring. And then if you can hold her so she doesn't turn, that would be great."

"I got it."

He smiled back at her. "Good. Now talk to her. Pet her. Love on her. Oh, and watch those teeth. I don't know what kind of woman she is. She might be the angry-in-labor kind."

"What does that mean?"

"Nothing at all. Just some are a little more temperamental than others."

"Nice. Real nice." She soothed the horse, telling the animal that not all men were so insensitive.

Reese smiled, but he didn't have time to comment. The horse relaxed, and he had a minute to do what needed to be done. He reached for the bent leg. The stable door opened.

"Need help?" Jesse stepped into the stall.

"I think I've got it."

"Looks that way. Hold up a second." Jesse put a hand on his shoulder. "Okay, let's get that baby out."

The two of them pulled the baby as the head and neck came out.

"Oh yeah, a nice little filly." Jesse patted Reese on the back. "Good job, Reese. It's good to know that Cheyenne will have a pro for a birthing partner."

"Birth partner?" Reese pulled off his shirt and cleaned the foal's eyes and nose.

Jesse moved him back. "Mama horse is done with our help."

"Yeah, I figured her for the temperamental type."

And then it hit him, what Jesse meant by *partner*. Jesse thought Reese would be in the delivery room when Cheyenne gave birth. He stepped back out of the stall and swallowed hard, thinking about that moment, about the reasons he wouldn't be with her. But then he wondered who would hold her hand.

"Cheyenne?" He turned, looking for her.

"She's gone. Sorry, I didn't think." Jesse sighed and let out a low whistle. "You sure know how to make a relationship complicated."

"Yeah, no kidding." He tossed his shirt in the trash. "I need to find a shirt."

"In the tack room there are a few spares." Jesse walked away. A few minutes later he handed Reese a shirt. "Do you mind pink?"

"Ha-ha." He pulled on the shirt. "Where'd Cheyenne go?"

"I think she went back to the apartment. You know, I think I'd give her some space. But keep an eye on her, Reese. Preeclampsia can be dangerous. If she starts having bad headaches, blurry vision or serious swelling, you need to call an ambulance."

This was one more thing to worry about and one more way he didn't know if he could help her. He leaned against the stall and waited for Jackson and Travis to walk through the door. He'd heard their trucks and knew that Cheyenne must have called everyone.

What would he do if something went wrong and Cheyenne needed more help than he could give her?

While his brothers took care of the mare and waited for the vet, he slipped down the aisle to the apartment. He rapped lightly. There was no answer. He tried again and still nothing. He opened the door and stepped inside, calling her name.

When she didn't respond, he walked to the bathroom and got cleaned up. She probably decided to go to her place to pack a few things. He sat down on the couch to wait.

Chapter Nine

The stable lights were all on when Cheyenne pulled back up and parked under the little carport at the back of the big stable. She'd done a little scouting earlier and realized that a back door led to the carport where she could park and walk right in through a sunroom and the art studio rather than walking through the stable.

Tonight it served her purposes because it meant avoiding the gang of Cooper men who were in the barn with the mare. She eased through the door with her suitcase and a bag of groceries she thought she might need. When she walked through the living room she jumped back, startled to see someone on the couch.

She walked a little closer, knowing who it was and not surprised to see him there. He had stretched out and fallen asleep. His boots were on the floor next to the table, and he'd tossed his hat on a nearby chair. She giggled because he'd managed to find a clean shirt and it was bright pink.

For now, she wouldn't run him off. He was cute. She didn't want to be alone. Later she'd wake him up and send him to his place. She carried her groceries to the kitchen and started putting them away.

When he called out, she turned, thinking he must have heard her.

"I'm in the kitchen."

He shouted this time and the sound sent chills up her arms. Cheyenne walked back to the living room. He thrashed on the couch, kicking off the afghan he'd pulled over himself. He opened his eyes and yelled for someone. She couldn't make out the name.

Cheyenne sat on the edge of the trunk, her hands shaking as she reached to wake him. He turned, staring as if he saw her. But she knew it wasn't her face he saw. He was reliving what had happened in Afghanistan.

"Reese." She touched his shoulder. "It's me. It's Cheyenne. Wake up. It's a dream."

He didn't hear her. She moved from the trunk to the couch. Sitting next to him she pulled him close, cradling him against her. He wasn't a child. He was a grown man. She soothed him, brushing her hand through his hair. He wrapped strong arms around her and held tight.

"Reese, wake up." She swallowed a tight lump of emotion in her throat.

"Cheyenne." He brushed a hand across his face. "I'm sorry."

"You don't have to be sorry."

"I should have warned you." He leaned back, soaked with perspiration, his eyes closed. "I have nightmares."

"About Afghanistan?"

"Yeah. I can't get past this feeling that I should have known or I could have stopped it from happening. Each time I have the dream I warn them too late."

"You couldn't have…"

He opened his eyes. "I know. But do the families know? The Bernards lost a nineteen-year-old son. Do they know that I tried to save their son? I would have given my life for his."

She started to tell him not to say that because if he'd given his life she wouldn't have him. But she didn't really have him. She had these moments with him—temporary moments. He wasn't going to be in the delivery room with her, being her partner, holding her hand. She closed her eyes and pushed aside Jesse's slipup.

It wasn't as if she'd expected Reese to be

there. That had never been the plan. It hadn't been part of their arrangement. If things had gone according to plan, he wouldn't have been home from Afghanistan when she delivered.

"Have you talked to them?" She cleared her throat. "The Bernards, I mean."

He smiled and shook his head. "Not really. And Mia asked the same thing."

"Maybe you should."

"They live in Oklahoma City."

She reached for his hand. "I'll drive you down there. Tomorrow."

"I have an appointment in Tulsa tomorrow morning."

"I know. And after that appointment, we can drive down to Oklahoma City. We'll call the Bernards. Reese, it might help them to see that you're moving forward with your life. It might help you to let go."

"I don't see how." He leaned forward, resting his elbows on his legs. And she rested her hand on his back.

"I don't know, but I think it might."

"You're an amazing woman. He should have seen that in you." He sat up and pulled her close. "I see it."

"Reese."

She whispered his name, and then he silenced

her with a kiss. She closed her eyes. A kiss had never made her feel like this—like the most beautiful woman in the world. Reese's hands were on her face, and he cherished her with every touch.

"I'm going now." He stood but leaned for one last kiss. "Because I'm not going to mess this up, Cheyenne. Whatever this is, I don't want to take it for granted. You're too amazing to take for granted."

She watched him walk to the door, and then she sighed and leaned back on the couch. Amazing... She'd never been called that, not once in her life.

And he was willing to walk away—for her. He was not going to take advantage of their situation. He was nothing like Mark.

After a few minutes she opened the door that led to the stable. The lights were still on, but the only one in the stable was Jackson. He saluted by lifting his hat, but then he turned his attention back to the mare.

"Is she okay?" Cheyenne took a few steps into the stable.

"Yeah, I think she will be. I'm not sure what happened with her, but she has a pretty serious infection. The foal is good, though." He stepped back. "Want to see her now that she's dry?"

"I'd love to."

Jackson motioned her over. "She's a beauty. We had hoped she'd be dark like this."

"She's definitely beautiful." The dark-coated foal had sidled up to her mother and pushed at her belly, searching for something to eat.

A car door slammed. Jackson smiled and looked like a guy in love.

"That would be my wife, Maddie, and our daughter Jade."

"I haven't met them, have I?"

"No, they were in Branson for the past week— a going-back-to-school trip." He met his wife at the door. The two hugged and then headed back to the mare, arm in arm. A teenager pushed between them, her smile huge.

"Oh, hi." Maddie Cooper smiled and held out a hand to Cheyenne. "You must be Cheyenne."

"Cool beans." Jade laughed a little. "Reese is going to be a dad."

"No, Reese isn't. He…" She didn't know what to say.

Jackson slipped a hand over the girl's mouth. "She knows, but she can't help but stir things up when she gets the chance."

"I'm sorry. Geesh. But it would be a great story to tell when I go back to school next month." Jade snorted and flipped her blond hair as she moved past the adults to look at the foal.

Maddie Cooper shook her head. "She's incorrigible. She gets it from him."

"A family trait," Cheyenne commiserated. "I should go. I just came out to check on the mare one last time."

"Is Reese okay?" Jackson had a syringe and a bottle of medicine. "Sorry, ladies. It's time to give our new mom a shot. And the baby, too. I hope you don't have needle phobias."

"No phobias." Cheyenne watched him fill the syringe, and then she remembered he'd asked about Reese. "Does he have nightmares often?"

Jackson flicked the needle. "Sometimes he does. It's gotten a lot better. There are flashbacks, too. But he's learned some techniques for dealing with them. He carries pure peppermint, something about sniffing it, and he has an MP3 player with music."

"Peppermint and music?"

He smiled and went back to work on the mare. "I'll let him explain."

"Of course." She leaned in and watched as he smoothed a place on the mare's neck and gave her the injection.

She walked back to the apartment and sank into the soft leather of the couch. Lamplight cast a soft glow and a candle burned, making the room smell like fresh-baked cinnamon rolls. She thought about needing Reese. And then she let herself believe that maybe they needed each other—at least until they could be strong on their own.

Reese hadn't believed Cheyenne would hold him to the conversation of the previous evening, but she did. As they were driving to Tulsa the morning after the foal's birth, the morning after one of his nightmares, she'd picked up his phone and told him to call the Bernards.

He'd taken the phone and held it for a minute. "I don't know."

"I think you do. This is the right thing to do. If they don't want to see you, they'll tell you."

So he made the call. The Bernards were more than happy to meet with him. They wanted a chance to talk to him and had hoped he'd call. So after his counseling appointment, they headed south. A short time later the truck slowed to a stop and the GPS announced that they'd reached their destination.

"Here we are." Cheyenne turned off the truck. The radio continued to play softly and would until one of them opened a door.

He whistled and let out a long breath. "I'm not sure if I can do this."

"I think you have to."

"Pressure much?"

"You made me move into the stable apartment. Sometimes we have to push a person to do what's best for them."

"Okay, we can do this." He reached for the door handle but paused. The song on the radio was about realizing you're in love and being surprised. He turned to where he knew Cheyenne was still sitting.

"We should go." She opened her door and the song cut off.

He smiled and got out of the truck. "Chicken."

"I'm not a chicken." She took his hand and hissed, "Stop making this about us."

"My apologies."

They walked up the sidewalk. He heard the screen door open. Cheyenne's hand on his tensed.

"Reese Cooper?" a woman asked, choked with tears.

"Yes, ma'am."

And then her arms wrapped around him. He heard footsteps behind her and a throat cleared. "Let him go, Wanda."

She turned loose. "I'm so sorry, it's just that

you're the one we have left. I'm so glad to see you doing so well. And is this your wife?"

He reached back for Cheyenne's hand. "Yes, this is Cheyenne."

She didn't immediately step forward. He heard her start to say something. Finally she moved to his side. "Cheyenne Cooper."

"It is so good to meet you both." Wanda Bernard hugged him again. "Come in, please."

He nodded and reached. Cheyenne placed his hand on hers, and they walked through the front door. His mind kept replaying what Mrs. Bernard had said. He was the one they had left.

One of seven, he alone had survived. He thought about the six other families and realized what she'd meant by that. In a sense, maybe he'd become the son, father, brother to all six families who had lost soldiers. Up to this point, he'd just considered himself a reminder of what they'd lost.

As he got stronger, he might try to visit each of the families. It might help them all.

"Have a seat." Mr. Bernard's voice was gruff, but Reese understood the kind of gruffness that helped a guy hold it together.

Cheyenne whispered, "This way," and she led him to a sofa. They sat down together, husband and wife—temporarily. He had married her thinking she needed something he could give her: stability. He laced his fingers through hers and said a silent thank-you to the One who had known the future and had known that they would need each other.

"You have no idea how much this means to us that you're here." Mrs. Bernard had returned. He heard the clink of a glass hitting a coaster. "I have tea. Do you need something to eat? I have cookies. Or I could make you a sandwich."

"No, you don't have to do that." Reese reached, touched the cold glass and lifted it to his lips. The tea was sweet and lemony. He set it back down, feeling with his other hand to make sure he didn't miss the coaster. "I wanted to come by and check on you. And to tell you how sorry I am."

"You don't need to be sorry, Reese." Mr. Bernard had leaned close. His voice still had that gruff tone, but it had softened. "We know what happened out there that day. We know how you tried to help our boy. We know it isn't easy for you."

Reese rubbed a hand across his forehead and nodded. "It hasn't been easy. I keep thinking back, to signs that might have warned me that something was ahead of us."

"There's no cause for you to do that, Reese. You can't fight an enemy that you can't see."

"No, ma'am, not usually." He lifted the tea again. "I just wish I could have. I would give anything to give you your son back."

A rough hand touched his. "The best thing you can do is keep living your life."

"Yes, sir." Reese reached for the hand of the woman sitting next to him. "We've taken enough of your time. I just wanted to stop by and tell you how sorry I am. And I wanted to tell you what a great boy you raised. When the rest of us were down, he kept holding on to faith."

He heard a sob and he hoped he hadn't said the wrong thing. Cheyenne gave his hand a light squeeze.

"I'm sorry. I don't mean to hurt you. I only wanted to tell you what you already know. Your son had more faith than most of us will ever have. And I'm sorry for your loss."

"We know, son. So are we." Mr. Bernard cleared his throat. "But we know our boy wouldn't have wanted you to feel this way. He was a little guy when the Trade Centers got hit. From that moment on, he said that someday he'd serve his country and help to keep it safe. He did what he wanted to do. And he knew Who he trusted in. He's with his God now."

Reese stood and he did what felt right. He saluted. And after a tight hug from the Bernards, he left their home feeling a little stronger, a little lighter. Once they were on the road, he realized that Cheyenne had been very quiet.

"Chey?" He smiled at the nickname. Shy she wasn't, but he liked the shortened version of her name.

"I'm here." She sobbed a little. "I told you that would be good for you."

"Yeah, it was. But what about you? Are you okay?"

"I'm good." She sniffled. "I loved those people."

He smiled and then laughed a little. "There are tissues in the console between the seats."

"Thanks." She fiddled and he heard the console flip up.

"Find them?"

"Yeah." She blew her nose and he cringed.

"Feel better?"

"Oh, be quiet. You can't do something like that and expect me, a super emotional pregnant woman, not to cry."

"No, I guess not." He reached to turn down the radio. "Thank you for going with me to do that. I really couldn't have done it without you."

"Because you needed me to drive." She gave a watery laugh. "Sorry, bad joke."

"Very bad. And other than the driving, I'm glad you were with me."

"You're welcome." She sniffed again. "I'm sorry for teasing you."

"I really don't mind. Laughing is better than the alternative."

She sobbed a little. "Stop. Here I am crying and you're making comments like that."

"I'll stop." He smiled, though. He couldn't help but think about kissing her. Teary cheeks and all, he wanted to pull her close and kiss her senseless. Yeah, he'd come a long way in two months.

"I guess we go home now?"

"I think so."

Home. He liked it when she said it that way.

It wasn't home for good, though. She'd stay in Dawson to raise her son. She'd run the old barbershop and she'd go to church at Dawson Community Church. She'd be around. After the birth of her son, she would no longer be in his life.

Chapter Ten

Cheyenne found Reese in the arena. He'd been doing more around the ranch for the past week since their trip to Oklahoma City. She smiled, watching him on the back of a green broke gelding. She now understood that *green broke* meant not really broke. She cringed thinking about the fact that he had saddled a horse that really hadn't been ridden much.

But he looked good on that horse. She leaned against the wall and watched him on the big gray. He had his hat low. His jeans were ragged at the hems, and his boots were old and scuffed. He turned the horse in a tight circle, used his heels and sent the animal forward. She held her breath when the horse bucked a little.

"Reese." She meant to call out, but his name came out in a whisper. But he heard her and turned in her direction.

"Chey?" He rode the horse a few steps, stopped and dismounted, landing easily on the ground. "You okay?"

"I'm good. I'm just worrying about you."

He led the horse forward and stopped in front of her. "I can't see, honey, but I can feel. When he starts that nonsense I can feel it through the saddle. He hunches a little and hops. It's about balance."

"I suppose a man who used to ride bulls knows a little bit about how to ride an animal that bucks."

"A little." He grinned, and then he leaned through the bars of the gate and motioned her forward. She leaned and he dropped a sweet kiss on her mouth. "Stop worrying."

"I have to worry. I'm a woman and it's what we do."

"Worry less. Trust more."

"I just wanted to let you know that I'm leaving. I have a doctor's appointment." She bit down on her bottom lip because she knew that her worry was evident in her tone. "It's good, though."

"Let me go with you." He reached, found the latch on the gate and opened it.

"I can do this on my own. I should do this on

my own." As much as she wanted to stand firm and resist his attempt to be involved, she couldn't.

"Of course you can. But it's more fun when you have someone with you. You were with me when we went to the Bernards last week. You drove me to my counseling appointment."

"I don't mind."

"And I want to go with you." He led the horse through the gate. "Let me put this bad boy back in the field and we'll take off."

"Thank you."

"You're welcome."

She stopped in her apartment to grab her purse and met him at the truck. She'd gotten used to driving his big Ford F-250. It pulled out smoothly and headed down the road, the radio playing country music. Reese pulled off his hat and tossed it in the backseat, and then he brushed his fingers through his hair.

Cheyenne glanced in his direction and then refocused on the road.

"I didn't know you had an appointment today," Reese said as they drove through Grove.

She cleared her throat and shifted as the truck slowed. "I didn't."

"What's going on?"

"I haven't felt well all day. And earlier my head started to ache. I called Dr. Richards."

"Cheyenne, why didn't you tell me?"

"I did tell you. You're here, aren't you?"

He shook his head. "That isn't what I meant. You should have told someone, told me."

"I've been taking care of myself for a long time, Reese."

"I know, but you don't have to. You have a family."

She downshifted as they drove through town. "No, Reese, not really. I have a borrowed family. They're yours, not mine."

"And that borrowed family cares about you. You need to stop pushing people away."

It was a habit. She could have told him she'd been pushing for as long as she could remember. From the day she heard her parents whisper that they should have trusted God more and waited, she'd been pushing. More than twenty years had passed since that moment when she'd realized she'd become their mistake.

They should have waited for Melissa—their birth daughter.

"I can't discuss this. My head hurts. I'm very close to being sick."

"Are we there?"

She nodded as she pulled into a parking space. "We're here."

"Do you need help getting in?"

"I'm fine."

She met him at the front of the truck. He had the white cane in his hand, and they walked side by side up the sidewalk. A young family came out of the office, moved to the side and watched them enter the building.

"In here." She touched his arm at the door that led to her doctor's office.

Reese took her hand and they walked in together. Cheyenne smiled at the receptionist who looked up from her paperwork when they entered.

"I have an appointment with Dr. Richards."

"Yes. She said to bring you right back. You can both go in."

"No, that's okay." Cheyenne led Reese to the waiting room. "I can go in alone."

"I want to go with you. If there's a reason, I can leave. Cheyenne, this isn't the plan we made in Vegas, but it's what we have now. I'm not going to sit out here while you're in there alone."

The door that led from the waiting area to the exam rooms opened. A nurse smiled at Cheyenne. "Are you coming back?"

"We're coming back." Reese reached and found her arm. "Let's go."

Cheyenne nodded, and together they followed the nurse back to an examination room where she told them to take a seat. Her heart thudded hard as she thought about what the doctor might say. She had six weeks to go. She thought about the baby being in danger. She thought about delivering alone. Her head pounded and she closed her eyes.

"It's going to be okay." Reese stood next to the exam table where she sat. "You're not alone."

"I know." She lifted his hand and kissed it. "Thank you for being here."

"I wouldn't be anywhere else."

The door opened and Dr. Richards walked in. She was young, sweet and always smiling. But today she looked concerned and that wasn't what Cheyenne needed.

"Cheyenne, I'm glad you came in. I'm going to take your blood pressure and we'll go from there. But how are you feeling right now?" As she talked, the doctor looked at Cheyenne's feet and then her hands. She lifted a light and checked her eyes. "Blurry vision?"

"No, just the headache and a little nausea."

The nurse walked in and picked up the blood pressure cuff. Cheyenne held out her arm. Reese moved back a step, but his hand rested on her back, lending support, strength that she desperately needed.

"One-thirty-five over eighty," the nurse spoke quietly to the doctor.

"Okay. That's a concern. You've been taking the meds?"

"Yes."

Dr. Richards drummed her fingers. "Still working at the salon?"

"Yes."

"Well, right now I'm not inclined to put you in the hospital. I think we'll try bed rest for a few days and see if that brings your blood pressure down. I'll contact Jesse and see if he can help monitor that for us."

Cheyenne exhaled a pent-up breath and nodded again. "Okay."

"So, you have a ride home?"

Cheyenne looked at Reese. He brushed a hand through his hair and shook his head. "I'll make a call."

"We'll get a ride."

"I'll take care of it." Reese walked to the door and had his phone out as he stepped into the hall.

Cheyenne closed her eyes and took a deep breath. Nothing was going the way she planned—not even her heart.

Reese opened the door to the stable apartment. He knew that Madeline had gotten Cheyenne situated on the couch after they got back from town. He had gone to the house for food because she didn't have a lot to choose from, and he knew his mom had homemade chicken noodle soup. She kept it in the freezer for situations like this.

"Soup's on," he called out as he walked through the door. No answer. "Marco?"

"Polo," she whispered from the living room.

Reese set the soup on the table and walked back to the living room. "You okay, Polo?"

She laughed a little and he sat down in the chair across from the couch.

"I'm good." She moved on the couch. "I don't know if I can stay on this couch and let everyone take care of me."

He thought about that and then he nodded. "Yeah, it isn't easy."

A long silence followed. "I'm sorry."

"No, don't be sorry. I'm just agreeing with you. It isn't easy to be in this position, where you need to be taken care of and there's nothing you can do about it. There's no way to change what's happening, though, so you accept the help and make the best of it."

"I could be on this couch for the next few weeks, Reese. I can't begin to imagine just lying here, letting everyone wait on me. I can't help but think that I should have stayed in Vegas. This wasn't part of the deal, you having to take care of a pregnant woman."

"I'm glad you're here." He pulled his phone out of his pocket. "I also think you should call your family."

"Reese, not now. I've talked to them, but I'm not sure any of us are ready for this. It's been a lot of years."

"I'm going to say something pretty tough, Cheyenne."

"Okay."

"You didn't let them make that choice. You left and they didn't have a way to reach you."

There was silence. He wanted to see her face, see her expression, and he couldn't. He moved from the chair to the trunk in front of the couch. He held out his hand and her fingers laced through his.

"I need to see you." He leaned close and she drew his hand to her face. He touched, felt her sorrow, felt the tears trickling down her cheeks. "I'm sorry."

"It isn't your fault. You're probably right about me taking the choice away from them. But, Reese, they have a daughter, a real daughter. I was always the mistake."

"You're not a mistake." He brushed the hair

back from her face, letting the silky strands slide through his fingers.

"Yeah, I'm pretty sure that's what I am. They rushed out to adopt when they thought they couldn't conceive. You rushed to the altar with someone you thought you'd never see again."

He leaned to kiss her. He gave her one sweet kiss and then he backed away.

"You're not a mistake. You're strong and beautiful. And sometimes what we feel at one moment isn't what we will always feel. Maybe they had a moment when they thought something or said something, but now, years later, they have other feelings."

"I'll let them know. Just not yet."

He put the phone back in his pocket. "Are you hungry?"

"Starving."

"I'm going to heat up Mom's chicken soup."

Her hand touched his cheek. He didn't move away. She brushed her fingers across his cheeks and then through his hair and then to the back of his neck. He leaned and kissed her one last time before getting up.

"Soup." He smiled and walked away.

He had the soup in the microwave when someone knocked on the door. He waited for Cheyenne to answer. When she didn't, he walked through the room, found the door and opened it.

"It's me," Jesse said.

Reese motioned his brother inside. "I think she's asleep."

"She is. And is that chicken soup I smell?"

"Mom has it in the freezer."

"Good to know." Jesse walked away. "I'm going to take her blood pressure before I head home for the night. I'll be back in the morning to take it again."

"Thanks." Reese eased through the room, found a chair and sat down.

"Cheyenne, can you wake up?" Jesse asked. Reese smiled because Jesse had always sounded like a doctor. Even as a kid, when one of the younger siblings got hurt, Jesse kept cool and took care of things.

"I'm awake," Cheyenne muttered, still sounding half-asleep.

"Good." Jesse rummaged for something. "I'm going to take your blood pressure. But I want you to remember to call if the headache gets worse, if your vision blurs or if you have abdominal pain."

"Got it," she whispered, fear trembling in her tone.

"No driving yourself," Jesse said with force, and then the blood pressure cuff pumped up.

"What is it?" Reese asked after a long minute of waiting.

"It's lower than it was at the doctor's office. I'm not sure what the plan is, but she needs someone here with her tonight. Are you staying?"

Reese stood to walk his brother to the door. "No, Heather will be over when she gets back from Tahlequah."

"Got it. Strange, but okay." Jesse touched his arm as he brushed past. "Take care of her."

"Will do." Reese closed the door after Jesse left and then felt his way back to the kitchen for the soup. He touched the dining room chairs and the bar before circling around to the microwave. "Ready to eat?"

"Yes. I can get it, though."

He walked around the corner of the kitchen. "Cheyenne, I can do this. It's a bowl of soup. You're not getting up."

He found a deep bowl and filled it with soup. He also searched the cabinets and found a tray. He slipped the legs of the tray over his arm, picked up the soup and a spoon and walked into the living room.

"See how amazing I am."

"You are." She reached and took the bowl from him. "Are you going to eat?"

"Not yet. I need to go help with a few chores." He set the tray over her lap. "Will you be okay while I'm gone?"

"I'm good. I have my cell phone. I'll call if there's a problem."

"I won't be far away."

Reese walked out the door and into the stable. He heard Travis singing and he laughed. "You still can't carry a tune in a bucket."

"I'm an amazing singer," Travis responded, and then Reese heard boot steps heading his way. "You going to help feed?"

"I had planned on helping Gage. He has some calves up that need shots."

"I think he and Jackson already took care of that."

"Fine, I'll help you feed. Did the Mortons stop by for that gelding of theirs?"

"Yeah, they were pretty happy with him, too." Travis moved past him. "I already have feed in the wheelbarrow. I need to get a round bale moved out to the bulls in the big corral."

"I'll feed. Do you have the ropes tied?" Their system for feeding was if the stall door had a rope tied to it, Reese knew there was a horse that needed to be fed.

"Yep. Thanks for feeding. I'll be back in thirty."

"Got it. Hey, where's everyone at?"

"I think they're getting ready for that bull ride in Kansas. Mom has a friend out there, so she's even going. I guess you'll be staying here with Cheyenne."

"Yeah. I'm not going to leave her alone."

"I didn't think you would. Hey, do me a favor. Don't ride that green gelding while we're gone."

Reese walked away, bumping the side of the wheelbarrow in the process. He reached to steady it.

"Reese, man. I'm sorry."

Reese grabbed the handle of the wheelbarrow. "Let me be the one who decides what I can and can't do."

"Yeah, I know." Travis thumped him on the back as he walked past. "I'm going to get that round bale."

"I'll see you later. Oh, when are you leaving for Kansas?"

"Not for a couple of days. Everyone else is leaving in the morning."

"Good to know." Reese waited for Travis to walk away, and then he started forward with the wheelbarrow. He had a system. He started at the far end, went down one side and then the other. The ropes on the doors kept him from having to step into each stall to see if there was a horse inside that needed to be fed.

He'd fed the first three horses when the stable door opened. He turned, waiting for whomever to speak up. When they didn't, he took the lead. "Who is it?"

"Reese, sorry, it's Adam MacKenzie." The one-time pro football player had stepped closer. "I didn't expect to find you out here."

"What do you need, Adam?"

"I came to talk to you about the camp. I thought I'd give it another shot."

Reese nodded and touched the next stall door. There was no rope. He moved on. The next one had a rope. He scooped grain and dumped it in the feeder. Immediately the horse started crunching on his evening meal. Reese touched the hay to make sure the horse had plenty. The water was filled automatically.

"Tell me what you have in mind." A week or two made a big difference. When Adam first approached him, Reese hadn't been able to think past finding his way through the house.

"Okay." Adam followed along as Reese fed. "I want to try a one-week camp for kids with disabilities. I thought if I brought in counselors with similar situations the kids would see their limits differently. They would see people like yourself, moving forward and grabbing hold of your life."

"Right." He fed the next horse, and then he stopped because he could feel anger mounting. He wasn't sure why he felt angry.

Adam had married Jenna Cameron, an amputee. He knew how strong a person with a limitation could actually be. Adam's sister-in-law, Willow Cameron, happened to be profoundly deaf, so he'd witnessed people with disabilities achieving their goals.

"Reese, I know this is tough."

"I know you do." Reese finished feeding the last two horses in the barn and found the bench next to the tack room. He sat down and Adam sat next to him. "Tell me more."

"You're perfect for this program, Reese. Not only are you facing this with strength and faith but you have a counseling degree. You could really help kids who are struggling to adjust to their disabilities."

"Adam, this may come as a surprise, but I'm still struggling to adjust. I can't drive my wife to the doctor." *Wife.* He shook his head because that really hadn't been the thing he'd planned to start with.

"I know it's tough. And listen, Jenna is just a

mile down the road if you need to talk to someone who has been there—literally been there."

He turned toward Adam. Even though he couldn't see him, it helped to make that contact. "I appreciate that. And I'm glad you think I can do this."

"You've been riding, right?"

"Yeah, with help, I can ride."

"Reese, you are handling this. There are kids who really need a role model like you."

"I'll think about it." He stood up. "I have to check on Cheyenne and make sure Heather will be here soon."

"The camp will start in a month."

Reese pulled out his cane and unfolded it. He walked to the door of the apartment and paused. "Sign me up."

"Thank you. And make sure you call if you need anything at all."

He stood in the stable and listened as Adam walked away. A minute later the door clicked shut and he heard a truck start. Alone again he bowed his head and said a quick prayer that he wouldn't regret what he'd agreed to. And he prayed that Cheyenne would be safe.

He had called her his wife. He shook his head and walked back to the apartment. There were some things a guy just couldn't explain or understand. Sometimes he just had to go with the flow and do what felt right.

Chapter Eleven

Reese walked in from the barn. Cheyenne smiled and clicked off the TV. "Who was here?"

It had been a voice she didn't recognize. She wasn't really nosy, just bored—already. One day into bed rest and she was bored out of her mind.

"Adam MacKenzie from Camp Hope."

"Oh, yes. They've been to the shop for haircuts. His wife is really sweet, and they have cute kids."

"They're good people."

Cheyenne felt a little twinge and it wasn't a contraction. She was huge, swollen and hadn't brushed her hair all day. Jenna MacKenzie was sunshine pretty and as sweet as they come.

"Is she a good friend of yours?" Ack, she wanted to take back the words, but they were already said and she sounded like what she couldn't be: a jealous wife. "I'm sorry."

Reese sat down in the chair opposite the couch, a cute grin on his handsome face. He pulled off his sunglasses and slid them into his pocket. He did that with her, she noticed. Perhaps it was because he was comfortable, she thought. When he was around other people he kept the sunglasses on.

"I never dated Jenna." He cocked his head to the side a little and his grin softened. "I never dated a lot. I just thought when the right woman came along, I'd know. Besides, I wasn't fond of the drama when things didn't work out. Or wasting my time on a relationship that wasn't going anywhere."

"And then you married me." She laughed a little and so did he. "I'm sorry. This is probably way more drama than you counted on."

"It's drama but not the 'please take me back, I can't live without you' kind." He took off his cowboy hat and dropped it on the nearby table.

"Eww, is that how we women sound to you men?"

He smiled, and she could see why a teenage girl would plead to have him back.

"Sometimes," he answered. "I always kind of wondered why they'd work so hard to make one guy love them when there were plenty waiting to love them."

"Interesting thought." She leaned back on the couch and tried not to overthink what he'd said.

"Do you need anything?"

"No, not really."

"A glass of water?" He stood, the perfect cowboy, the real deal. And he had married her. She sighed and started to nod.

She caught herself. "A glass of water would be good. You know, you don't have to stay here with me."

"Do you want me to leave?"

She didn't have to think about that. "No, not really. And I got you sidetracked. You didn't tell me what Adam MacKenzie wanted."

He clicked the cane side to side as he made his way through to the kitchen. "He asked me again if I would help with Camp Hope. They want to do a weeklong camp for kids with disabilities."

"And you said?"

"I told him I'll do it." He returned with a bottle of water, opening it before he handed it to her. "I'm not sure what I can do, but I'll help if I can."

She took the bottle of water from his hand. He pulled the chair closer to the couch and sat down.

"You're not sure what you can do? Really?"

He grinned again. "You were a cheerleader in high school, right?"

"Are you kidding? No, I wasn't a cheerleader. I was far too dark and scary for that."

"You were dark and scary. How?"

"Literally, dark and scary. I went through an angry phase."

"You were goth?" He laughed and then he shook his head. "I would have loved to have seen you like that, with your blond hair and blue eyes. As a matter of fact, I'd love to see you right now."

His smile faded and she wanted it back. She crept from the couch to sit on the trunk in front of his chair. With a tremble inside she reached for his hands and lifted them to her face. "I think you see me better than anyone ever has."

"I know I do." He spread his fingers over her cheeks and moved them across her face and then down to her mouth. His finger drifted across the sensitive skin of her lips. "I know you're the most beautiful woman I've ever seen."

"I would like it if you would kiss me," she whispered as she leaned close.

"I think you're supposed to be on bed rest," he teased, leaning to touch her lips so briefly it could have been a butterfly flitting away.

Cheyenne moved her hands to the back of his head and pulled him close. "Please kiss me."

He pulled her gently to him and kissed her. Gently he held her. Gently he took her heart. She didn't know how to get it back, but she knew that in time he would break it into a million pieces.

"Cheyenne, I'm not sure if I can let you go." He tangled his fingers in her hair. "I'm not sure if I want to let you go."

"Reese, don't. This isn't real. These moments are happening because of what we're going through."

"Isn't it?" He reached for her hand, and she knew he felt her tremble. "Isn't it real?"

"Emotion. We're both going through so much."

"Right. Of course you're right." He heard a car pull in. "That would be Heather coming for the night shift, and you need to be on the couch."

"Stay for a little while."

He smiled and shook his head. "No, I think I'll head on back to my place. But Heather will be here if you need anything."

She touched her fingers to his, a light touch that didn't hold him, but it kept him at her side for a moment. "I'm sorry."

"I don't know why. We both knew what we were doing, Cheyenne. We made an arrangement and for a minute it felt like…" He shook his head. "But you're right, this is just emotion."

She watched him walk to the back door and greet his sister. His profile was strong. His smile shifted his features, made him more amazing. He lifted a hand to wave before he walked out the back door. Heather locked the door behind him.

"How are you feeling?" Heather took the seat Reese had vacated, and she put her feet up on the trunk.

"I'm good. Jesse came by earlier to take my blood pressure. It's lower than it was."

"Cheyenne, I've known my brother a long time. My whole life, actually." Heather smiled and made a face. "I know when something is up. I know when he's hurting. And I can tell by your face that you're not in the best place."

"We're fine. I think it's just too much…being together like this. We hadn't planned on being this close. I should have thought about that before I came to Oklahoma. If I'd stayed in Vegas, this wouldn't have happened."

"You would have been alone." Heather patted her arm. "Let me get you some ice cream."

Cheyenne smiled but she shook her head. "No, thanks. Reese has fed me several times already and I'm stuffed. What I want is to get up."

"No can do." Heather reached for the remote and flipped on the TV. "Want to watch a chick flick?"

Romance. She wrinkled her nose and shook her head. "No, thanks."

"Western?"

Cowboys. "You go ahead. I'll rest."

"Mystery." The mysteries of men… She smiled and Heather frowned. "Anything?"

"I'm not much of a television person. I haven't had much time, working two jobs the past few years."

"What did you do in Vegas?" Heather turned off the TV.

"I waited tables." Cheyenne reached for her bottle of water and Heather slid it close for her to pick up. "And I was a dancer. Those ballet lessons finally paid off."

"Oh." Heather bit down on her bottom lip. "Did you enjoy it?"

Cheyenne laughed and shook her head. "Nothing in life prepared you for this, did it? I mean, who would have thought a Cooper would marry a showgirl."

"Really, Cheyenne, give yourself a break. And us? We're not perfect."

"You look perfect to me."

"It's an illusion. We fight. We make mistakes.

We hurt each other. No perfect here. So did you enjoy your dancing career?"

"No, I didn't enjoy it, but I made decent money. Most of which my husband took to the casino."

"That's rough."

"Not as rough as finding out we were never married." There was more to the story, but it was the more that Heather didn't need to hear, that no one needed to know. Like how it felt when Mark put her in a car and drove her to an abortion clinic. She closed her eyes against the memory.

"Cheyenne, are you okay?"

She looked up and smiled. "Of course I am."

"You looked like you were in pain. Jesse said to call if you had any pain at all."

"I'm not in pain." She closed her eyes. "I'll take a nap and you watch whatever you want. And don't be afraid to go to sleep. I promise I'll be okay."

She would be okay. She had always been okay. Somehow God would get her through this, and she would survive and raise her little boy. She slipped a hand to her belly and remembered how angry she'd been when she took that first pregnancy test. She'd called this unfair.

She'd cried. She'd lost hope. And God had sent Reese Cooper.

After she no longer had Reese, she would still be okay because she would still have God.

Reese climbed in the truck with Gage after a pretty sleepless night. He'd just gone out to check on Cheyenne. Rachel Johnson, their pastor's wife, had brought a casserole and offered to sit with her while Reese ran a few errands.

"You look rough." Gage shifted into Reverse and backed the truck out of the parking lot.

"Thanks. I feel pretty bad so it's nice to know I look the same."

"Did you think I would start playing nice?" Gage laughed. "I'm the bad one, remember?"

"Yeah, right. Where's our little brother Dylan? At least he's decent and has a good bedside manner."

"Dylan is meeting the folks in Kansas. And you're right. He's pretty near perfect."

"Is that anger I hear? What's up with the two of you?" Reese clicked his seat belt in place and waited for Gage to answer. If he would answer.

"Dylan is the one with the problem, not me."

"What does that mean?"

"Nothing much. But if I have to knock him down again, I will."

"Gage, why don't you go ahead and tell me what's going on?"

The truck picked up speed. "Nope."

"Fine."

"Where are we heading?"

Reese turned down the loud rock music on the stereo. "Camp Hope."

"Okay. Fasten your safety device and put your seat in the upright position."

"I'd like to get there in one piece."

"Kidding. Stop taking everything so seriously." Gage laughed. "I would never speed."

"Right."

A few minutes later they pulled up the long driveway to Camp Hope. Reese felt pretty certain they'd gotten there in record time. When they came to a stop he turned toward his brother.

"One of these days, Gage, life is going to catch up with you."

"Yeah, it probably will. Fast trucks, loud music, faster living."

"Good thinking. Glad you listened to Mom and Dad."

Gage snorted. "You know, I'm about tired of being a Cooper. I'm tired of everyone thinking that being the kid of Tim and Angie means being perfect."

"No one said you had to be perfect. You can make mistakes without going crazy."

"Maybe I want to go a little crazy." Gage sounded pretty serious. "Can you get a ride back to town?"

"Seriously, you're going to drive me out here and dump me?"

Gage laughed. "Yep. Don't worry. Adam just walked out of his office. I'm hitting the road. I'm not sure when I'll be back."

"Gage, be careful."

"Will do." Gage tossed something at him. Reese caught his hat and shoved it on his head. "Reese, I really am glad you're doing okay."

"Thanks." Reese stepped out of the truck and closed the door. As he stepped back, the truck moved past him and down the drive.

"Was that Gage?" Adam walked up behind him.

"Yeah, I think. Or some alien inhabiting his body. I came out to talk to you for a few minutes, but it looks like I'll need a ride home."

"No problem. Are we going to talk about the camp?" Adam touched his arm. "There's a picnic table over here. It isn't too hot yet, and the fresh air feels pretty good after being inside."

"Yeah, it does." Reese pulled the sunglasses

out of his pocket and slid them on. "What is up with my brother?"

"Growing pains?" Adam stopped him in front of the picnic table. "Right here."

"Thanks." Reese sat down on the bench of the picnic table. A cold nose hit his hand and he smiled. "Jenna still raising collies?"

"Collies and German shepherds."

"Nice." He ran his hand over the thick coat. "About the camp… I like the idea, Adam. But I have something else I'd like to bring up."

"Shoot."

"A retreat for soldiers returning from combat. A place where they can get away for a few days or a week and not have to worry about fitting in, trying to make everyone else comfortable with what they're going through. They can be around people who have been there. They can talk, maybe have group counseling sessions. A place where they can find a way back into life."

Adam whistled. "I like it. And what if we go one step further and do a family weekend once in a while?"

"I have some money that I need to invest. I'd be happy to help build on. Whatever you need."

"I think this is a deal, Reese." Adam reached for his hand and shook it, his grip tight. "I think Jenna is going to love this idea."

"Good." Reese let out a breath, and then he relaxed with the warm sun on his face and the familiar scent of drying summer grass. In the distance he could hear horses whinnying and kids playing. He could picture it because he'd seen this a thousand times in his life. "It feels good to be here."

"What if we set you up an apartment on the campus?"

Reese nodded. "I might take you up on that. I don't need much."

"Have you forgotten you have a wife?" Adam's tone teased but Reese heard the concern.

What did he say? Cheyenne planned on staying in Dawson after her son was born. He wanted people to accept her, to include her. He didn't want them to think the two of them had walked out on their marriage.

"Cheyenne and I won't…" He started over because Adam could handle the truth. "Adam, I married Cheyenne to give her insurance and a way to get back on her feet."

"So the marriage…?"

"…will be annulled after her baby is born."

Again Adam whistled. "How do you feel about that? The two of you seem pretty tight."

"We're friends."

"Gotcha." Adam touched his arm. "Jenna is

in the arena. Do you want to tell her what we're going to do?"

"Let's go." He stood and with the cane in his right hand he walked with Adam. New territory meant new obstacles. It meant being unsure of what was in front of him. He had no idea what lay between them and the barn. "As we walk could you give me the lay of the land?"

"Yeah, of course. We were at the office, a single-wide trailer. You know that to the south of the office, that's left after you come off the porch, is the chapel. We're heading that way and then we'll go left again. We'll go past dorms and then we'll be at the stable and the arena. There's another dorm past the stable."

"Thanks. That helps."

It was a long walk and he didn't have to stop. All of those weeks in physical therapy had gotten his body back in shape. For the most part, he'd gotten past the pain.

"Right here." Adam turned him toward the barn. "This door leads to the stable. It's set up pretty much like the one at Cooper Creek but maybe not as fancy."

"Gotcha. Hey, do you still have that mechanical bull?"

"Yep. You want on?"

Reese followed him through the barn. "Maybe soon. At least if I fall off, it can't chase me down."

"Hasn't happened yet." Adam stopped. "Jenna, we have company."

From the other end of the barn he heard Jenna yell that she'd be there in a minute. And then she squealed, "Reese."

"In the flesh." He smiled and they started walking toward her. When she reached them she grabbed him in a hug that took him by surprise. "Is that you?"

She laughed. "It is, and I'm so glad to see you out here. You're going to join us?"

"More," Adam announced. "He has a plan for a retreat that gives soldiers a place to regroup."

"I love it." She hugged him again.

And then his phone rang. He smiled an apology and pulled it out of his shirt pocket. "Hello."

"Reese, it's Jesse. We have Cheyenne and we're taking her to the hospital. Her blood pressure is pretty high, and I think we might need to transport her to Tulsa."

"I'll meet you there." He hung up. "Adam, can you get me to the hospital? Jesse is taking Cheyenne in."

"Of course. Let's jump in the farm truck. It's parked here, and we won't have to go looking for my keys."

"Thanks." He reached and Jenna's hand touched his. She placed his hand on her arm and walked him outside. Man, it hit him head-on. He couldn't get to Cheyenne without help. He couldn't get anywhere without help. Almost thirty years of independence yanked right out from under him. He took a deep breath and exhaled slow.

At least he had people who were willing to help out. The positive for the negative. He wished the replacement thought helped. It didn't mean too much today.

"Climb in." Jenna opened the door for him. "And call me when you know something."

"Will do." He closed the door and Adam already had the engine cranked. Within minutes they were on the road toward Grove.

"I'm sure she'll be okay," Adam said as they drove. "My sister had preeclampsia, and even though it gave us a scare, the delivery and the baby were fine."

"Thanks." It was not his baby and not really his wife. He knew the reality of the situation. They all knew. No one was fooled into thinking he would be going to his wife or bringing home a new baby.

As they pulled up to the hospital, it felt every bit like his wife and his son in there, in jeopardy.

He'd been praying hard like they were his. He'd been sweating it all the way to town, worrying about them.

The truck jerked to a stop. "Here we are."

Reese got out and it was hard, waiting for Adam to join him. He wanted to get in there, get to her side.

"This way." Adam took him by the arm.

"Way to feel like a man." Reese muttered, fighting a huge dose of righteous anger that he had to work to get past. "Sorry, I appreciate you, Adam. It's just this. The situation makes me want to hit something."

"I have a punching bag back at Camp Hope. You could take up boxing."

Reese laughed and then he got it. Adam wasn't kidding. "Yeah, you know, that might be good. A way to take out my frustrations."

"Exactly." Adam stopped walking. "We're looking for Cheyenne…"

"…Cheyenne Cooper," Reese finished.

"Right this way." The nurse walked off and Reese stood there.

"Another moment that I love. Where did she go?"

"This way." Adam guided him down the hall.

"Reese." It was Jesse's familiar voice. Reese had never been so glad to hear his brother.

"Where is she?"

"Down here. I'll take you."

"I'll let you go with Jesse." Adam patted him on the back. "Call when you know something. And we'll all be praying."

"Thanks and I will." He reached and Jesse took his arm. "How is she?"

"Not good. Reese, we need to get her on a Medi Flight to Tulsa, but there isn't an available helicopter. Her blood pressure is high and the baby is in distress. Dr. Richards isn't here. The other obstetrician is in surgery. And our hospital isn't equipped with a NICU."

"Okay, get a helicopter, Jesse." He jerked away from his brother. "We're Coopers. That should mean something. We should be able to take care of her."

"Keep your voice down." Jesse pulled him to the side. "I called Gipson Cross. He has a private copter that he uses to get back and forth from his spread here to the airport in Tulsa. It just so happens it's sitting at his place and not in use. His pilot is on the way there, and we'll transport Cheyenne by ambulance to meet him."

"I'm going with her."

"We're both going with her." Jesse still had hold of his arm. "She needs you."

"I know." He touched the wall, felt it ground him. "Where is she?"

"In here, with Heather." Jesse touched his arm. "Five paces and you're at the door. Put on a smile and let her know that everything is okay."

Reese nodded and walked straight ahead, using the wall as a guide. When he walked through the door, he heard silence and then his name on a broken sob.

How had it happened this way? He'd had a simple exit strategy and now it had all come pretty unraveled. The woman in that bed was counting on him. As much as he wanted to be someone she could count on, he knew she needed someone who could walk through a hospital without being told how many steps to take and which way to turn.

But it was his name she'd cried. He wanted to be the man she could count on.

Chapter Twelve

Cheyenne couldn't help the sob that escaped when she saw Reese walk through the door. When all of this had happened she'd only been able to think about him being with her. But in the last hour another thought had replaced that one.

If she had her baby today, her marriage would be over. The agreement ended with her son's birth. Reese would walk away. She would go back to being Cheyenne Jones. Another sob welled up, and she buried her face in her hands.

"Cheyenne, I'm here." He sat down on the edge of the bed and reached for her hand. She took a deep, shaky breath as his hand held hers tight.

"I know. I'm sorry—I just—when you left I didn't..."

"Shh, it's going to be okay. We're going to get

you to Tulsa. Think about the baby." He stroked her hand, calming her. "Stay focused on your son and how much he needs for you to be calm."

She nodded and sobbed again. "I'm trying."

"You're good. The baby is good. There are people all over this county praying for you."

"That's good, I need it."

"Don't we all." He smiled and she closed her eyes as his fingers brushed through her hair.

"I'm not ready to have a baby."

He laughed a little. "I don't think that's up to you."

"He isn't ready."

"He's going to be ready."

A nurse entered and behind her, paramedics entered with a gurney. "Reese, they're here to take me."

"I'm not letting you go alone."

She held tight to his hand. "I can't do this."

He took off his sunglasses and leaned close. "Look at me."

"I am." She smiled. "I like looking at you."

"They must have you medicated." He stroked her cheek. "I'm here. You're good. Keep your hand on your belly and remember who is in there and what he needs from you."

"Who made you so smart?"

He kissed her cheek. "Lessons learned, sweetheart. Lessons learned. I'm right here behind you."

As they loaded her she felt faint. She clawed at the blankets and tried to hold on, the way Reese had told her to, but everything went dark. "Jesse?"

"Right here. You're good, Cheyenne. We'll have you to Tulsa in no time."

"Jesse, I'm afraid. It doesn't feel right."

He touched her shoulder. "I know. And we don't have time to talk. You're going to be in Tulsa in thirty minutes. They're waiting for you."

"Jesse." She shuddered.

"Hang on, Cheyenne. Reese is here and we're heading out."

She closed her eyes as they moved her from the bed to the gurney on a count of three. Within minutes she felt herself being loaded in the back of an ambulance. Reese wasn't with her. She opened her eyes and flicked her gaze around the sterile confines of the ambulance. An attendant smiled and talked into a radio. He put a hand on her arm.

"We'll be at the helicopter in four minutes. Hang tight, Mrs. Cooper."

She wasn't Mrs. Cooper, not really. She wanted

to tell him that she was a fraud. She'd never been who she thought she was—ever. She'd never been the person who anyone wanted to keep—ever.

But her baby wouldn't feel that way. She did what Reese had told her to do. She put her hand on her belly and felt her little guy move inside her. She felt him kick. She smiled and tried to pretend it didn't hurt.

Where was Reese? She breathed through a contraction and yelped when the paramedic moved her arm, shifting the needle in her vein.

"Sorry." He touched the tape and made sure it had remained in place.

"Where'd Reese go?"

"He can't ride with us. Dr. Cooper will take him in his truck."

She nodded but it didn't feel any better. She needed someone. She thought back to being a child, being sick, and her mom sitting next to her bed, trying to comfort her, hugging her tight when she cried. But Cheyenne had pushed her parents away because she'd heard that conversation. She'd known how they felt about adopting her. She had pushed them out of her life.

She had done it. She closed her eyes. If she got through this she would apologize. She would make amends for not listening when they'd tried to stop her from going to Vegas. She'd make amends for the horrible way she'd treated them.

"We're at the ranch." The attendant readied her for the move from the ambulance to the helicopter. "You're going to be wheeled out on the gurney, but then you'll have to ride sitting up in the helicopter because it's a private aircraft, not medevac. But Dr. Cooper will be with you to monitor your condition, and we're going to try and bring the equipment with you."

"I understand." But another contraction wrapped around her middle. "Should it hurt like this?"

The paramedic nodded. "I'm afraid so. You're in labor, Mrs. Cooper. And your blood pressure is pretty high."

"I'm okay." She breathed, keeping her hand on her belly. "Where's Reese?"

"I'm right here." He looked in the open door. "We're good to go."

She nodded but she saw something in his eyes that worried her. She saw fear. She saw panic. "Reese?"

"Yeah?"

They helped her out of the ambulance, and she didn't have time to ask him if he was okay. But of course he was. He was Reese. He handled everything.

And then they were at the helicopter. She tried to breathe, to be calm, but the blades were swirling and everything in her body hurt. She held tight to Reese as they helped her into the reclining seat in the helicopter. Reese sat next to her. Jesse sat in the seat facing her. The pilot greeted them as they buckled up.

"You okay?" Jesse leaned and looked at her.

She nodded. She had to be. She wouldn't think about the possibilities, about seizures or stroke, about losing her baby. She closed her eyes and recited verses she had memorized as a little girl. These long forgotten verses seemed to have been waiting in her memory to be recalled when needed most.

Next to her she heard Reese recite, "The Lord is my shepherd, I shall not want…"

She reached for his hand. The helicopter blades were spinning fast, and the big machine rumbled and started to lift. She opened her eyes and saw Jesse shift his attention to Reese.

"Reese, peppermint." Jesse reached and shook his brother. "Hey, stay with us."

Cheyenne shifted her attention to the man at her side. But he wasn't Reese, and he obviously wasn't with her. He stared straight ahead, as if he saw something she didn't, something horribly frightening. His hands gripped the arm of the seat, and he said something she couldn't hear.

"Reese!" she shouted his name and then she slugged him because she didn't know what else to do. He turned to face her, his eyes wide with fear.

"I can't do this." He reached for his seat belt. "I can't go back."

"You aren't going back!" Jesse shouted. "Get the vial out of your pocket and focus on where you're at."

Cheyenne held tight to his arm. "Reese, I need you with me."

He nodded. "I'm here."

He reached into his pocket and pulled out a vial. He took off the lid and sniffed. With his right hand he held her hand tight. She glanced at Jesse.

"Why peppermint?"

Jesse shrugged. "The scent is strong and it's something real. It gets his focus off the flashback. Now, Reese, ground yourself."

She kept hold of his hand and slowly he came back to her. This was the fear she'd seen in his eyes. This was the panic. He'd already prepared for the panic attack. He knew he'd have a flashback. But he'd gotten on the helicopter with her anyway.

* * *

Reese held tight to Cheyenne's hand, because she needed him. He wouldn't let himself be pulled back, to the faces of his guys. He pushed aside the thoughts that haunted him, thoughts of their eyes, their faces. They had needed him. He hadn't been able to help. And then there was the second explosion, right before the air support got to their location. Then there was nothing.

"Reese!" Jesse shouted his name. "Cheyenne is next to you."

"Cheyenne." He held her hand. He knew her touch. He knew her scent. He knew her skin. It was soft beneath his hands. He could do this.

"You with me?" Her voice came to him, waking him from something like a living nightmare. Flashbacks were real, though. He knew because he'd been having them for two months. But they were never this bad.

"I'm with you." He leaned close. "I'm with you."

She held tight to his hand. "I'm not letting you go."

"Good idea." He breathed through the fear and focused on the woman next to him, needing him. He hadn't been able to save his guys. He could save her.

"Reese, how are you?" Jesse yelled from across the helicopter.

"Good. Not great but good. Not feeling like much of a man."

"Don't say that." Cheyenne lifted his hand to her cheek. "I need you and you got on this helicopter for me."

"We're not there yet." He tried to smile but he couldn't, not yet. The helicopter blades where pounding and he could hear the pilots. But then he heard weapons being fired and an explosion. He shook his head. The weapons weren't real.

Reality. God. Cheyenne. Jesse. He moved his hand and found what he sought: the rounded evidence of a baby coming into the world. He kept his hand in place, feeling when the baby kicked and moved.

"I'm good." He breathed and Cheyenne covered his hand with hers. "This is very good. We should call your parents."

She whispered that they could do that when they got to Tulsa. Her voice sounded weak. She sounded afraid.

"Cheyenne, hold on. Okay?" He moved his hand to her arm. "Jesse, is she okay?"

"She's good. The contractions are pretty steady." Jesse paused for a minute. "Her blood pressure is still high."

"Cheyenne?" Reese held her swollen hand. "We'll get through this."

"I know." She sounded weak. "And then what happens?"

He knew what she meant by that but he couldn't answer. What would she say if he said, "Stay together and make this work"?

Right now, with him shaking in his boots, probably wasn't the best time to put his heart on the line.

The helicopter landed. He didn't know where they were or what would happen next. Next to him Cheyenne froze and then her body started to shake beneath his hand.

"Jesse?" He held tight to Cheyenne's hand. "What's going on?"

"Back up." Jesse pushed him to the side as the door opened and warm air rushed in at them. "Get a gurney. She's seizing. We have a pregnant female, thirty-four weeks gestation, blood pressure is…"

Reese sat back, not hearing everything, unable to see anything. The commotion swirled around him, and then Cheyenne was gone and he was alone. He sat there for a second, unsure. A hand touched his arm.

"Reese."

"Dad, what are you doing here?"

"Jesse called before you all left home and told us to meet you here."

"Good. Now you can tell me where they've taken her and how we get there."

"They're taking her right in to surgery," his dad explained as they crossed to the doors that led from the helipad into the hospital.

"She shouldn't be alone."

"She won't be." His dad led him through the building. The air was cool, sterile. "I think your mom is waiting to go in with her."

"I have her phone. We should call her parents. I think they would want to know."

"Good idea." Tim took the phone from him. "I'll find their number and you can call them. You're her husband."

Reese brushed a hand through his hair and let out a ragged breath. "Yeah, the guy who can't be with her."

"This situation doesn't have clear rules, Reese. You married her, but you're not married. I don't know what to tell you, other than you're going to have to decide."

"I've already decided." He took the phone and walked off. He'd decided that he loved her. He had also decided she needed more than him.

He held the phone to his ear while it rang. When it was answered he introduced himself and then he told Lori Jones that her daughter was in a Tulsa hospital. He gave the specifics and Cheyenne's mother cried.

"Tell her we love her. We'll be there as soon as we can."

"I'll tell her."

Reese stood in the hallway, waiting. His dad finally came back.

"We can wait down here. Jesse just had a nurse come out to tell us that the seizing has stopped. They have her on oxygen, and they're going to start the cesarean as soon as they can get scrubbed in."

"Good to know." Reese held his dad's arm. The cane was folded and in his pocket. It didn't do a lot of good when he didn't know where he was or where he was going. He hadn't realized until then how much he'd come to rely on it.

"Here's the waiting room." His dad led him through a door.

Reese felt for a chair and sat down. After a few minutes he stood up, wanting to pace. Cheyenne was having a baby—not his baby, he reminded himself. But it didn't really matter to him that it wasn't his. "Is there coffee in here?"

"Yeah, I'll get you a cup."

Reese sat back down. "I'd appreciate that."

A minute later his dad placed the coffee in his

hand. "It's instant, but that's what you get from a vending machine. Welcome to fatherhood. Bad coffee, worry, doubt. Sound about right?"

"Yeah." But he wasn't a dad. He sipped the coffee and waited…and waited. "I can't take this."

"It's only been ten minutes." His dad laughed.

"Easy for you to laugh."

"It isn't like I haven't been through this a few times."

"You went in with Mom. You didn't wait in a waiting room."

"Yeah, I did." His dad sighed. "How was the helicopter?"

"Other than the flashback, minor panic attack and then Cheyenne going into seizures, wonderful."

"Exciting." Tim patted his arm. "Finish the coffee. We'll go lurk in recovery."

"I'm done with the coffee." He stood and waited for his dad. "Let's go."

They walked down the hall and waited outside a door. Reese paced in the area that he knew, keeping track by using the wall as a guide.

"You're going to wear a hole in the floor."

"I have to do something." He paused and listened. A door had closed inside the recovery room. "Is that her?"

His dad stepped next to him. "Yeah, it's her. Jesse is heading this way."

Reese took in a deep breath and waited. The door opened. Jesse stepped close, touching his arm. "She's good, but she isn't out of the woods. We have her on a heart monitor and oxygen, not a ventilator."

"Okay, what does this mean? Is there something permanent?"

"Not that we know of. She seems to be responding to the meds. Before we put her under, she followed our commands. She's good, Reese. Preeclampsia became eclampsia. But she's going to get through this."

"What about the baby?" Reese moved closer to the door.

"We've taken him to the NICU. He's a little stressed and needs oxygen, as well as monitoring, but he'll be good."

"You're sure?"

"Yeah. Come on. Cheyenne will need to see your pretty mug." Jesse led him through the door. "Try not to say anything stupid, like about the annulment."

"Right, thanks for thinking I'm callous."

"I don't. I just know you, brother. I know how your mind works and your big sense of right and wrong. Right now you're having a truckload of doubt, and you think you can't be the man she needs."

"You can get a job for a psychic hotline if this doctor business doesn't work out." Reese thought about Adam's punching bag.

"You know I'm right. I saw it on your face back in the helicopter."

"Good, thanks. Now where is she?"

"This way." Jesse didn't move forward. "She loves you. It's all over her face."

"Jesse, not right now."

"I know." Jesse led him to her bed, placed his hand on her arm and told him to take care of her.

"Reese?" Cheyenne's voice was soft and teary.

"Right here. You're okay."

"I don't feel okay. I feel weak." She shivered beneath his touch. "Where's my baby?"

"He's being taken care of." He reached for a chair and sat down next to her. "They had to take him to the NICU. He's going to be fine, though. He just needs help breathing right now."

"I need to see him." She moved beneath his hand. "I need to hold him. I haven't even held him."

"I'll see what I can do." He started to stand but she had a viselike grip on his arm.

"Don't leave me alone."

"Mom is here. She'll stay with you, and I'll go

check on the baby." It was her baby. He leaned, found her face and brushed the soft tendrils back. He kissed her cheek. "I'll make sure he's okay and be right back."

"Mr. Cooper." A nurse stood behind him. "I can take you to the NICU to see your son."

He started to correct her but he didn't. Instead he took the arm she offered and followed her down the hall. He tried to keep track of steps, of turns. His mind whirled, wondering where he would end up—not today but tomorrow, next week.

They stopped. The nurse moved his hands to the cold metal of a sink. "Wash your hands and I'll get you a gown."

"Thank you." He slid his hand around the edge of the sink, found the levers and turned on the water to wash his hands. He remembered how simple a task it used to be, to wash his hands. He remembered how simple it used to be to walk down a hall and get where he needed to go.

He shook off the thoughts as the nurse walked up behind him, touching his shoulder.

"Here we go." She helped him into a gown, putting it on over his shirt.

"Once again, thank you." He managed a smile.

"You're welcome." She took his arm and led

him through the room. "Here he is. The bed is open and heated. You can touch him."

"How is he?"

"He's only five pounds, but he'll be okay. His lungs are strong and so is his heart. It's just the stress of the last twelve hours or so that has made him a little weak so he needs extra help breathing."

"She'll want to know what he looks like and if he has hair." He knew because women always wanted to know about those things. "Ten fingers? Ten toes?"

"Well, Reese Donovan Cooper has very little hair. It's blond, like his mom's. Sorry, Dad." She touched Reese's back. "And he's very cute."

"I'm not..." And then he paused because he didn't want to tell her that he wasn't the dad. "She named him after me?"

"That's the name she gave us." The nurse patted his back. "Surprised?"

"Yes, surprised." He stepped closer to the bed. "I can touch him?"

"Of course you can. I'll help you out." She guided his hand, and he felt the tiny arm of the little boy with his name, and then he felt his head, his feet. "My brother was in the military in Iraq."

He turned to face her, wishing he could see her face. "Afghanistan."

"My brother lost his leg." She moved his hand to the baby's tiny hand. "He's a lawyer now."

"That's good."

"What are your plans?"

"Surviving." He said it without thinking and then realized the truth in that statement. "And helping other veterans find a place to regroup. We're going to use Camp Hope in Dawson."

"That's amazing." She touched his arm. "He's awake and his little eyes are on you."

"When will Cheyenne be able to see him?"

"I'm not sure. I think as soon as the two are stable."

"Are you a praying person?" he asked her.

"I am and I'll pray for your wife and son." The nurse had stepped away, but she moved back to his side.

Now was the time for truth, but he couldn't face it. The little fingers curled around his finger. The tiny grasp might as well have been around his heart. There were a lot of things that could take a man to his knees. Most included force. Reese shook his head, amazed that a baby had that kind of power.

Chapter Thirteen

Cheyenne awoke with a start. Her whole body ached. Her head spun. She opened her eyes and turned, searching for Reese...always for Reese. She saw him asleep in the chair next to her bed. She'd been moved to a room. She didn't remember.

But she had a baby. After his birth she'd watched as a doctor and nurse took care of him, measuring him, weighing him, examining him. And she'd waited for the moment when they would put him in her arms. But instead they'd left with him. They'd taken him away before she could touch him.

"Reese."

He nodded and opened his eyes. "I'm here."

"I know." She wanted him to always be there, but she wouldn't be like the girls who had begged him not to leave them. "What day is it?"

"Same day, different hour. It's Thursday evening."

"How is my baby?"

"He's good." Reese moved in the chair. He sat up and then stood. She watched him stretch and then he walked to the bed. "Cheyenne, his name..."

She touched the hand that rested on the rail of the bed. "I wanted to name him after you. You've done so much for us."

"Thank you. I just— I had no idea."

"What does he...?" She stopped and closed her eyes tight. "I'm sorry."

"No, it's okay. I knew you would want to know what he looked like, so I asked the nurse." He stroked her fingers and he smiled. Her heart wrapped around that smile, memorizing it and how perfect it made this moment. "He has blond hair—not a lot but some. It feels like down. They say his eyes are blue like yours, and the nurse who is an expert, it seems, says the color will stick. And he's small, Cheyenne. They have him off the respirator and on oxygen. That's a good thing."

She moved in the bed. "I have to go to him. I need to hold him and be with him."

"No, you need to stay in bed so that you can get healthy and be there for him. Cheyenne, this is serious. You have eclampsia and you had a seizure before they could do the delivery." He ran a hand down her arm. "I'll keep an eye on him and you'll see him soon, but you need to take care of yourself, too."

"I need to hold my baby." She hadn't wanted to cry, but tears trickled down her cheeks and emotion tightened in her chest. "I need to see him."

"I'll have Mom take me down to get a picture of him. And you have company waiting to see you."

"Company?"

"Yep. So hang on and I'll get them. And I'll be back soon with the pictures."

She didn't want him to go. She reached for his hand, but he already had his cane out and walked easily toward the door. A minute later she heard footsteps and quiet voices. She closed her eyes and waited.

"Cheyenne." The voice was familiar. She opened her eyes, stunned, unable to take a deep breath.

"Mom."

The woman in front of her had aged. So had her father, who stood at the door, waiting. They were older. She was older. But their smiles were genuine. She didn't know what to say. It had been ten years.

"I'm sorry," she sobbed, covering her face with her hands.

"Shh." Her mom stepped close to the bed and then gathered her in a long-forgotten hug, forgotten because for so many years Cheyenne had pushed aside the good memories and held on to the bad. She had kept the memories that validated her anger. She'd forgotten the pleas, the love, the forgiveness.

"We're so glad you're safe. And we're sorry for anything we did to hurt you."

"I…" She shook her head because now wasn't the time to tell them what she had believed. "I'm glad you're here."

"So are we. And you have a beautiful son and a wonderful husband. We're so happy for you."

"Thank you." She held tight to her mother's hand. "You were right."

"It doesn't matter. It was never about who was right. It was about wanting you to be safe and happy." Her mom touched her hair. "And I'm so glad to see this."

Her blond hair. She smiled because it had taken a lot of work to get the black dye out of her hair.

They talked for a while, and then she heard footsteps in the hall and people talking, laughing. She glanced past her parents as Reese walked through the door with his mother.

"We have photographs." Reese held up the camera. "I took them myself."

"Funny." Cheyenne reached for the camera, her hand shaking. She held it close and smiled at the image of the tiny baby boy. He was stretched out in a bed, tubes and wires all around him. It was *her* baby.

"Isn't he a handsome guy?" Jesse walked through the door with another doctor behind him. "This is Dr. Reaves. He delivered Reese this afternoon."

Cheyenne looked from the picture to the doctor who approached her bed. He held out his hand. "Hi, Cheyenne. Nice to see you conscious."

"I owe you all so much." Cheyenne glanced around the room. Her gaze lingered on the man next to her and then on Reese.

"You did the hard work." Dr. Reaves patted her arm. "Now, what you need to know is that your blood pressure is still relatively high. I'm not making any moves to get you out of this bed for now. Tomorrow, if everything goes well, we'll put you in a chair and take you down to see your little boy. And if he continues to improve, the next day we'll bring him up here to room in for a couple of days."

"I can handle that plan."

"Good." Dr. Reaves smiled at everyone. "But don't expect to feel great—not for a few weeks."

"I understand."

"If there's anything you need, let the nurses know and I can always be contacted."

"I appreciate that."

He patted her hand one last time. "Enjoy that little boy of yours. He's strong and healthy. He just has a few small obstacles."

"Obstacles?" she whispered after Dr. Reaves left. Jesse stepped forward.

"He's had a hard couple of days. He's small, and oxygen is helping him to rest, to not work so hard."

"I understand." She covered her eyes with her hands. "I'm just so tired."

"Rest." Jesse touched her shoulder. "Take a few minutes to visit with your family and then get some sleep."

She nodded, still holding her hands over her face, trying to pull it together before she lost it completely. It was too much to think about: her baby, somewhere in this hospital, needing her. Reese was one step away from walking out of her life and she had no right to hold on to him.

"Cheyenne, we're going to our hotel. We'll be

back in the morning." Her mom leaned over and kissed her cheek. And then her dad touched her head, stroked her hair back. Cheyenne nodded but she couldn't respond.

After they left, Reese stepped forward. He messed with the rail on the bed and finally got it down. Cheyenne watched, not sure what to say.

"Reese?"

"I need to hold you." He sat on the edge of the bed. "But I don't want to hurt you."

She leaned into his side, grimacing past the sharp pain in her abdomen. His arms wrapped around her.

"You're going to be okay."

"Am I?"

"I promise." He rubbed her arm, holding her close.

"I'm afraid."

"So am I." He kissed her cheek and then held her for a long moment. "Better?"

"Yes." Amazingly so. A minute in his arms and she felt like she could get through the next twenty-four, even forty-eight, hours.

"I'm going to be here. I'm not going anywhere."

She nodded, still resting her head on his shoulder.

She sighed when he moved away, returning to his chair next to the bed. She thought about mentioning the annulment. For his sake she had to bring it up. She couldn't—yet.

Reese woke up early and found a nurse who could help him make his way to the NICU. Cheyenne was still asleep. He knew she'd rest better if she woke up and he had a report on her son. The nurse led him to the bed where his namesake slept. A pediatrician joined them. She introduced herself.

"How is he this morning?" Reese reached, found the baby and stroked his arm.

"He's good. He's breathing on his own but we're giving him oxygen indirectly. There's a tube near his face. He really is very healthy." The doctor reached past him, adjusting something. "He woke up when he heard you. He must recognize your voice."

Reese nodded and found the hand that curled around his finger. How did he keep them in his life? He stroked the little hand and said a prayer.

"We'll wean him off the oxygen this evening. We'll monitor his blood oxygen levels to see how he does, as well as his heart rate. But he's clear of infections. His urine output is good. He's doing very well." The pediatrician rested her hand on his shoulder. "Do you want to hold him?"

He did, but he couldn't. "I think Cheyenne should hold him first."

"Then sit here awhile. I'll pull up a chair. You can talk to him and touch him. These babies really need contact with their parents. That's what helps them get stronger faster."

He heard the chair being pulled close. "Thank you."

"No problem. Stay as long as you want."

Reese considered telling her he wasn't the father. Instead he sat next to Reese Donovan Cooper, touching his small hand and telling him what a lucky kid he was going to be. He promised to teach him to ride and rope someday. Maybe they would go riding together.

After a long time he walked out of the NICU. In the hall he stopped to get his bearings. Right turn, down the hall and to the left. He tapped his cane against the wall to keep himself on track.

As he walked down the hall, footsteps approached. "Reese?"

He paused, unsure of the voice. "Yes?"

"It's me, Mrs. Jones."

"I just checked on your grandson." He smiled and waited.

"He isn't your son, is he?"

Reese kept walking, swinging the cane in front of him. She stepped beside him.

"I think you should have this conversation with Cheyenne." He stopped. "Is there a place where we can sit?"

"I'm sorry, yes, of course. Over here." She took his arm and led him a short distance. "Here's a seat."

"Thank you." He felt for the seat and she took the chair next to his. "Cheyenne needs time to tell you her story. And ours. But trust me. She needs you."

"I wish she had trusted us more. I know what she thinks. I know she believes we were sorry we adopted her. We probably said things we shouldn't have. But we love Cheyenne. We never wanted her to leave."

"I think you'll have to tell her that yourself."

"What about you, Reese? Do you love our daughter?"

He smiled and stood. "I have to get back to her room. She's going to want an update on her son."

"Reese, I'm not sure what's going on, but I hope you stay in her life."

"Me, too." He took a step, ending the conversation.

"I'll walk with you."

"Thank you."

They walked the short distance to Cheyenne's

room and her mom touched his arm. "You go on in. I know she's wanting to see you and we were just in with her."

He nodded, touched her arm as he stepped away and then he walked through the door into the quiet hospital room. The TV was on and the volume was low. He touched the bed and Cheyenne's hand covered his.

"I'm awake. Have you seen him?"

"I have. He's doing really well. They're going to try weaning him off the oxygen this evening. How are you feeling?"

"They woke me up and made me stand. It wasn't pleasant."

"I'm sure it wasn't." He reached, found a chair and pulled it close. "Maybe they'll let you go down to see him."

"I hope so." She sighed. "Reese, we have to talk. It's time to talk."

"No, it isn't. You're still recovering and we have time."

"But I can't do this. I can't pretend you're always going to be here for me."

"There are people who will always be there for you, Cheyenne. Not everyone in life is going to let you down." He brushed his thumb across her hand. "I'm going to do everything I can for you."

"I'm too tired, Reese. I'm too tired to fight. Too tired to have dreams. I want to get my baby and go home."

"Where's home?"

She turned in the bed. He heard the rustle of sheets, her body moving. "I'm not sure right now."

A noise in the hall interrupted the conversation. Reese smiled because he knew that voice, knew those steps. "Granny Cooper is on her way."

Cheyenne laughed a watery sounding laugh. He touched her shoulder and she rolled back toward him. "I'm sorry for being so emotional."

"You have a right to be emotional."

High heels clicked on the floor behind him. He waited, smiling, because he knew his granny had business to attend to if she was wearing heels. And he could guess what the business would be about.

"Reese, Cheyenne. Don't you two look happy?"

"We're tired, Gran." Reese smiled up at her. She patted his shoulder. "You're out early, though."

"Well, of course I am. I have a new great-grandchild. And you need to shave."

"I'm sure I do." He ran a hand across his

cheek, feeling three days of not taking time
to shave.

"Well, I'm not here to nag you about shaving.
I'm here because I have a gift for Cheyenne."

Reese stood. "You can have my chair."

"No, thank you." Granny Cooper mumbled
to herself for a minute. She crumpled papers,
made a few more noises and then, "Ah, there it
is. I thought I lost it."

"What is it?" Reese held out his hand.

"Not for you. For Cheyenne." Granny Cooper
pushed his hand aside. "Cheyenne, this was my
great-aunt's. It's been in the family for years and
I want you to have it. I must admit, I'm afraid
with all of these grandkids of mine I'm going to
run out of heirloom rings to give out, but I want
you to have this one because my great-aunt was
a remarkable lady who married a man she met
through correspondence. They had six children
and were together for sixty years."

"I can't take this ring, Myrna," Cheyenne
whispered, and Reese wondered which ring his
grandmother had given her.

"May I see it?" He held out his hand. Cheyenne placed the ring in his hand. He brushed
his fingers over the ornate setting. "The ruby-
and-diamond ring."

"It's a lovely ring." Granny Cooper patted his

arm. "You put it on her finger. She'll take it from you."

"Gran, I think you should let us discuss this."

"Discuss away."

"Without you." He slipped the ring in his shirt pocket.

His grandmother sighed big. "I didn't give it to you for you to put in your pocket, Reese. I want it on her finger."

"We'll discuss it."

"Now let me tell you something, grandson of mine. I've been amused by this situation. I've let you have your fun and pretend this isn't real. But marriage means something. It isn't to be entered into lightly. It's a binding thing, and when two people take themselves to that altar and promise to love one another, then they'd best do all they can to fulfill the vows."

Reese touched her arm, found her cheek with a little help from her and kissed it. "Gran, I can handle this."

"I hope you can. Now, you two talk, and I'm going to go see that little boy."

Reese listened to her retreating footsteps. The ring in his shirt pocket pressed against him, a reminder of a moment that shouldn't have complicated their lives to this extent.

"This is my fault." Cheyenne touched his arm.

"We'll work it out. But today isn't the day."

He leaned and her hand touched his cheek, guiding him to her. He felt her hair, her cheek, the softness of her skin. He kissed her as she cried salty tears.

When the kiss ended, he remained close. "You're going to survive this."

"I'm so afraid right now."

"I know, but this is where we're at. We have to figure out today before we can even begin to know what we'll do with tomorrow. And we do need to figure out what God has in mind before we make a big mistake."

What God had in mind? He didn't know how to make promises to her. A man had to be able to take care of himself before he could commit to a wife and child. And he was getting there. Each day got him a little closer to being the man she could count on.

A knock on the door pulled them apart. He turned, smiling at a visitor he couldn't see, but he did recognize the sound of the wheelchair being pushed into the room.

Cheyenne smiled at the nurse who pushed the wheelchair toward her bed.

"Mrs. Cooper, I'm here to take you down to see your son."

"I can see him?"

"You can. We're going to take this slowly. If you'll wait a minute, I'll have an aide help me get you out of bed. Mr. Cooper, do you want to push her down to the NICU when we're finished?"

Reese smiled and turned to Cheyenne, but she didn't know what to say or how to handle this moment. She ached for him.

"Of course I want to." He winked in her direction and pulled the white cane out of his pocket. "I'll be in the hall. Let me know when she's ready."

Cheyenne smiled as he walked out the door. She loved him. Her heart broke a little at the realization. Of course, she couldn't call it a realization, not when she'd been falling for weeks. Actually the fall had started in Vegas, continued through their letters, plunged rapidly when she got to Dawson.

He paused at the door, and she lifted her chin a little, letting go of any sadness the thought brought. For the time being he was her cowboy, the man who had rescued her. He was sweet and gorgeous and funny. He had confidence and a swagger that made the nurses turn and look.

For the time being...

"Okay, let's see if we can get you up." The nurse waited for the aide to walk in and close the door. "If you feel at all dizzy, you'll need to let me know."

"I will."

"We need to walk a little, too. I'm sorry about that, but it's important to have you on your feet and walking."

"I can do it."

She managed to get up, walk across the room and back as they instructed, and then they eased her down into the wheelchair. The nurse checked her blood pressure and it had remained high, but not at a dangerous level.

"This is really good." The nurse pushed her to the door. "Are you sure the two of you will be okay on your own?"

Cheyenne smiled back at the nurse. "We'll be fine."

"Okay then. To get to the NICU go down the hall, take a right and down to the next hallway where you'll go left."

"Got it."

The nurse pushed her through the door. Reese stood leaning against the wall next to her parents. When he heard her, he straightened and smiled.

"Ready to go?" He reached for her hand and she gave it to him.

"I'm beyond ready."

He patted her shoulder and then slid his hand to the back of the wheelchair and the handles. "Me, too. I'll leave it up to you to get us there."

"Okay, we're going in the right direction. Keep going and in about thirty feet we're turning right."

"Got it."

She concentrated on breathing and relaxing. Her baby had been in this world for twenty-four hours, and up to this point he hadn't seemed real because she hadn't seen him, touched him. She had worried about him and prayed for him, but now, finally he would be real in her arms.

"Turn left," she whispered as they got to the end of the second hall.

"You okay?"

"Nervous." It was for so many reasons but most of all because of reality.

"He's good, Cheyenne."

"I know he is. It's just…" She sighed. "It's just that now it becomes real. Everything becomes real. I'm a single mom with a little boy to raise."

His hand touched her shoulder. "You're going to be fine."

She nodded because she couldn't talk. Her throat ached with unshed tears and emotion so thick it kept the breath in her lungs. She clasped her hands together to keep them from trembling. She shook from cold and fear.

"Cheyenne, breathe."

"I'm breathing." It was only a little, though.

He laughed. "I can't hear you."

"Okay, I'm breathing." She took a deep breath. "I'm so afraid."

"You aren't alone."

She was alone. He was with her. Her parents were there. But she was alone. As she entered the NICU she realized how untrue that thought was. She sobbed as she saw him in the little bed, an oxygen tube close to his face and a clear tent over him.

She reached back to stop Reese. He stopped and moved to her side.

"I need to touch him." She looked around for a nurse. "Reese, I need to hold my baby."

"Okay, hold on. Let me get help." He moved away from her but paused and turned. "If I could see help."

He smiled and shook his head.

"A nurse is coming." She tightened her robe and tried to stand. Reese moved to her side, his hand clasping her elbow.

"Honey, I'm not sure if you should get up." The nurse reached for her other arm.

"I have to touch him." Cheyenne leaned close to the bed. "I need to hold him."

"Okay, you sit back down and I'll get him out of there for you. He's okay. You can hold him."

Cheyenne lowered herself back into the chair with Reese still holding her arm. She watched as the nurse moved swiftly, swaddling the baby in a blanket, moving tubes and wires. And then he was in Cheyenne's arms. His tiny little body fit against hers and he squirmed and scrunched his face.

"He's beautiful." She smiled at Reese, who had taken a seat next to her. "He's so tiny and beautiful."

"You know, we men don't really like to be called beautiful." He winked and leaned close. His hand touched her arm and slid down to touch her son. "We're handsome."

"Yes, you are." She whispered the word on a breath and he smiled. She recovered her senses. "I want to take him home."

"You can stay in the stable apartment, Cheyenne. There's more room."

Not right now. Not this conversation while they were together holding her baby. She didn't respond.

Reese sat back. "But you don't have to. Whatever you decide, I'll help you however I can."

"I know."

Don't leave me. She wanted to say it but couldn't. Rejection seemed to be a pattern in her life. For whatever reason, she was hard to hold on to. But her baby in her arms changed everything.

"Cheyenne..."

"Not now. Please, let's not talk now. He's beautiful and I want to hold him and be happy."

"I want you to be happy."

She nodded and when the nurse approached with a bottle she took it. She sat in the NICU, in that safe environment with soft sounds and soft colors and a cocoon of peace wrapped around her. She would be okay. She had faith.

Chapter Fourteen

Five days later Reese waited at the barbershop for Cheyenne to come in with the baby. Heather had driven them home while Reese made some last-minute changes to the shop, with Jackson's help. They put up the rest of the mini blinds, put a crib together and found a tiny bassinet. It was crammed into the back room, but she had insisted on returning to the barbershop.

"They're walking up to the door," Jackson said from across the room.

"Thanks." Reese finished putting the drill away, and he turned as the bell over the door dinged to announce their arrival. He unfolded his cane and walked toward her, stopping when she touched his arm.

"Reese." She sounded tired.

"We've been getting some work done for you. We thought it might make things easier."

"Thank you." She sighed a soft sigh. "We should probably talk."

He agreed. "First, you need to sit down. And I've arranged for Vera to have meals delivered to you so you don't have to worry about cooking."

"Don't, Reese." Her voice broke and the baby fussed.

Reese slid his hand down her arm, felt the tiny bundle in the blanket. Footsteps retreated and the door chimed again.

"I take it we're now alone?"

"Yes." She touched his arm. "Let's sit down. I really am exhausted."

They walked to the back of the room. Jackson had delivered a rocking chair and a wingback. He assured Reese the chairs didn't take up much room, and she'd have somewhere to sit other than the little room where her bed and the crib were.

"Reese, it's time for me to sign the annulment."

He heard the creak of the rocking chair. He sat down and listed.

"You've done so much for me. For us." Her voice broke on a sob. "And I can't keep doing this, taking advantage of you, pretending you're mine or that we will always be."

"Cheyenne, why don't we wait?" Forever.

That's what he wanted to say, but he didn't want to push her to stay in his life.

"No." The rocking chair creaked and the baby cried a little. "I have to feed him."

"Okay." He stood. "Cheyenne, I've never been sorry."

"Neither have I, but I know this isn't what we planned—me here, us together this way. It isn't fair to you that I barged into your life and stayed. You didn't have a chance to think about what you wanted." She touched his hand. "I think I'm going to stay with my parents for a while. My sister is married and has a little girl. There's so much of their lives I've missed out on."

"How will you get there?"

She laughed a little. "You have to stop taking care of me, Reese. Do you think I don't know what people say, about your heart and how you've always been too kind? You've always taken in strays. That's what I heard a man at Vera's say the other day."

Reese drew in a breath and he walked away. After a minute he walked back and squatted in front of her. "Whoever said that was dead wrong."

She touched his face. "Bring the paperwork over tomorrow and I'll sign it."

"Is that really what you want?"

"It's what I want." She sobbed, and he turned into the hand that still rested on his cheek. He kissed her palm and then he stood, leaning to kiss her.

"It isn't what I want," he whispered close to her ear.

She shook her head. "Go."

Reese stood and walked out of the building. The afternoon sun beat down on the sidewalk. He pushed on his sunglasses and waited to see if anyone would show up.

It made sense. Of course it made sense. He walked down the sidewalk, felt the stucco of the building and leaned facing it. He drew back his hand and stopped short of hitting the wall. Instead he pressed both palms against the warm stucco and let out a shaky breath.

"You ready to fight someone?" Jackson touched his back.

"Yeah, I'm ready to fight someone. And the problem is, I don't know who to fight."

"I'd rather it not be me. I'm an innocent bystander. Maybe you need to fight yourself, because it looks to me like you're giving up."

"She's going to Kansas to stay with her parents. She wants me to bring the paperwork over tomorrow so she can sign the annulment."

"Just like that?"

"She said she isn't a stray. That's what she heard someone say, something about me bringing home strays."

"Yeah, you've done that. A couple of kids in high school. A mangy dog from the side of the road. A horse that someone turned loose on government land. But I think that's a far cry from marrying a woman you met outside a Vegas diner."

"Oh, shut up." Reese walked off.

Jackson laughed. "You going to walk home?"

Reese turned and walked back to his brother. "No, I'm not going to walk home. But I am getting pretty sick of having to ask every time I need a ride to town. She thinks she's a stray? I can't even drive myself to town."

Jackson turned him toward the truck. "Head that way. And I think I know where you're going with this. You think you can't take care of a wife and kid?"

"Of course I can. Maybe she thinks this is too much." He pointed to his eyes. "Maybe she doesn't want to sign on for a lifetime of being my chauffeur, being my eyes."

He got in the truck and waited for Jackson to climb behind the wheel. Jackson started the conversation where they'd left off.

"Maybe the two of you need to sit down and talk, and be honest."

"Thanks." Reese leaned back in the seat. "I can't believe this is my life. A year ago I had this idea that I'd go into the military, serve my country for a few years, come home and settle down to ranching. Now what do I do?"

"Settle down and ranch?" Jackson downshifted and the truck slowed and turned. "So you do it a little differently. Maybe you need extra help. Maybe you work at Camp Hope and give a few kids a little hope. I can't tell you what will happen, but I know you and I know you're still going to live your life and you're still going to give back and be the man you've always been. With or without eyesight, you're that guy."

When they got back to the ranch, Reese had Jackson let him out at the barn. When he walked through the door, a horse whinnied. He walked down the aisle to the office and stepped inside. Country music played softly on the radio. The room smelled like pine and leather.

He found a chair and sat down. The barn was peaceful. It had always been the place he escaped to. As a kid he'd come out here to be alone and think. As much as he loved his siblings, being a Cooper meant finding a place to think without a dozen voices trying to help.

He used to think about things that were easy—girls, horses, how to stay on a bull. Yeah, it would be good to have those days back.

Cheyenne cuddled her baby against her and waited. Reese had said he'd bring the legal paperwork for her to sign. She'd called him two days ago. He still hadn't shown up. He'd told her he had a few things to take care of first. She'd explained that her parents were coming at the end of the week. She really wanted this done before she left for Kansas.

Her parents were supposed to be in Dawson that afternoon. She walked to the window and looked out. A car turned and came down the road. It was Heather's car. Cheyenne sighed and walked away from the window, back to the rocking chair Reese had brought to the shop for her. She sat down, her hands resting on the polished oak of the arms.

The door opened. Heather walked in, looking cool and beautiful as always. No one should look so cool, so together, on a hot day in August when the humidity had to be near one hundred percent.

"How are you feeling?" Heather set down two coffees. "I brought this from Vera's. She has a new coffeemaker and she's forcing coffee on everyone."

"I know. I had some the other day." Light moments like this made her feel like part of the community. And her parents were pushing for her to return to Kansas. They had asked her to live with them, to open a shop in the town she grew up in—to leave Dawson.

And why not? As soon as she signed the annulment, her marriage would be over. The ties with this town were based on what everyone believed to be a real marriage. She took that back. People did wonder why she was living in the barbershop and not at Cooper Creek.

Heather sat down in the chair next to Cheyenne. She sipped her coffee and pretended she didn't have something to say. Cheyenne knew she did.

"Spit it out." Cheyenne looked at Heather. "Go ahead. Say what's on your mind."

"Are you pushing my brother away because he's blind?" Heather set her coffee down. "It doesn't seem like you would be put off by something like that."

"What in the world are you saying?"

Heather leaned forward a little. "I think that's what Reese thinks. And I think people in town think the same thing. They think you married him, he got injured and now you're leaving because you can't handle being married to a blind man."

Cheyenne opened her mouth but words wouldn't come out. Heather raised a hand, stopping her.

"Cheyenne, I don't think that—at least not all of it. I know the truth about your marriage. People in Dawson don't. And of course Reese won't hurt you by telling them."

"That's good." She shook from head to toe, and she had to clasp her hands to keep them from trembling. "This isn't about Reese's blindness. I'm letting Reese go."

"What does that mean?"

"It means I shouldn't have come here. By coming to Dawson I pushed myself into his life in a way that we hadn't intended. It should have been easy. If I'd stayed in Vegas or gone anywhere but Dawson, it would have been easy. I wouldn't have..." She bit down on her bottom lip and tears burned her eyes. "I wouldn't have fallen in love with him, and it would have been easy to sign the papers annulling the marriage. Now it isn't easy, but I have to do it because he didn't sign on for this. He did a good deed, and he shouldn't be stuck with a wife and kid because of it."

Heather got up when the baby cried. "I'll get him."

"He's probably ready to eat." Cheyenne slipped past Heather to get a bottle out of the fridge. "He eats a lot."

"Cheyenne, you need to talk to Reese. The two of you are running from each other and you really need to be honest."

"I can't do it, Heather. I can't stay here after the annulment. I thought I could, but I can't. I don't want to be the person he regrets."

"You aren't." Heather leaned and kissed her cheek. She still held baby Reese in her arms, and he'd quieted when she'd picked him up. "You're a part of our family. None of us want you to leave."

"I'm the accidental part of the family. I'm the good deed."

"You might have started out that way, but things change." Heather handed her the baby. "But that's not for me to say. Talk to Reese."

A shadow drifted across the wall. She turned and saw her parents getting out of their car. "I can't. I've spent the past twenty years feeling like the mistake everyone made. I won't be Reese's mistake."

Heather shook her head and touched the baby's cheek again. "You're stubborn, and I hope you come to your senses before it's too late."

Cheyenne nodded and watched Heather walk away. Yes, she was stubborn. But being stubborn would keep her in one piece—eventually.

Reese unbuckled the chaps he'd worn riding with Adam MacKenzie and tossed them in the back of Jackson's truck. He turned, unfolded his cane and headed across the grassy area, back to the stable at Camp Hope. After two weeks, he'd gotten pretty good at finding his way around the camp. It was a good thing, because Adam had left him to go do something in the stable.

He'd not only gotten good at finding his way around but he'd also gotten good at not having Cheyenne in his life. He'd never taken the paperwork for her to sign, and then she'd left with her parents. She'd left a note telling him to mail it and she'd sign it and mail it back.

He hadn't. He was stubborn that way. He'd decided on one thing. He wouldn't let her go without a fight. He wouldn't let her go without showing her that they could work. They were good as a couple. Even if that hadn't been the plan when they'd started out at that wedding chapel in Vegas, that's the way he saw it. They worked.

"Where is everyone?" He tapped the side of the barn with the cane, found the door and walked down the aisle between the stalls. "Hey, don't leave me hanging out here."

He moved close to the wall. From the distance he heard voices. He couldn't quite place the office or tack room but knew they were on the right side. He kept going, swinging the cane back and forth as he went.

"Where are you guys?"

"In here." Jackson called out.

Nice answer. *In here* could mean anything. "Thanks for the great directions."

"Right here." Adam touched his arm. "We're in the arena. Did you want to ride that mechanical bull? We got it fixed this afternoon."

He had to think about it. For weeks he'd been pretty okay, no real pain. He shrugged. "I have a few minutes."

"Hot date?" Jackson walked up to them.

"Yeah, the women are knocking the door down." He touched the elevated platform where the mechanical bull was set up. "Besides that, I'm a married man. Remember?"

His wife was missing in action, but he did have the marriage license to prove they were a couple.

"Have you talked to her?" Adam asked as he

guided Reese across the arena, his hand loose on Reese's elbow.

"Not since she left town."

"I meant since she…" Adam stopped a little too quickly.

Reese turned, knowing Jackson had to be nearby and knowing that there had to be a silent conversation going on. "You know, this talking with your hands so I can't tell what you're saying is really unfair."

"No one said anything." Jackson cleared his throat. "Get on the bull and show us what you can do."

"Sure, I'll show you what I can do." Reese took a step toward his brother. Adam pulled him back.

"Take it out on the punching bag."

"Right." Reese turned, reached and found the mechanical bull. He climbed on and grabbed the rope. "I'll take it out on the bull."

Adam checked his hand. "You know, you could ask her out."

"Yeah, there's this problem, Adam. I can't drive over there and take her out." He sucked in a breath and pushed his hat down tight. "And my family forgot to tell me that she's back. She forgot to call."

"Maybe you're just not that cute." Jackson

laughed. "Hang on. Your bull is coming out of the chute."

Reese tucked his chin and raised his free arm. The bull started out with a whirling spin, then a rapid, mechanical buck. He gritted his teeth and held on through the pain in his back. He worked to keep himself centered. A quick turn and buck sent him off the back, flat on his back.

He lay there a minute, getting his senses back. He should have known Jackson wouldn't take it easy on him.

"Need a hand?" Adam walked across the padded platform.

Reese held up a hand. "Sure."

Adam pulled him to his feet. "You've still got it, Reese."

"Yeah, I don't think I'm going to be climbing on the real thing any time soon, but it did feel pretty good to be back on a bull—even one made out of a barrel."

"Ready to head to town?" Jackson asked, stepping close.

"Yeah. And you can drop me off at the barbershop."

"Maybe you ought to have more of a plan than that." Jackson led him off the platform.

"What would you suggest?" Reese unfolded his cane and took a few steps. "Man, that really hurts."

"What hurts?"

He stretched. "Nothing, I'm fine, just out of shape. I'd forgotten how hard you came off one of those things."

"At least you didn't hit the dirt floor of an arena." Jackson walked next to him. "So maybe you ought to try a little romance. That's something the two of you haven't had a lot of."

"Yeah, maybe."

"Or you could just storm in, pick her up and carry her back to Cooper Creek." Adam laughed as he gave his advice.

"You guys are a lot of help."

He walked away because any advice they could give would probably land him in serious trouble. He'd probably get better advice from Gage. He laughed at that. No, probably not from Gage. Or Blake. Or Jesse.

He was going to have to handle this one on his own.

"So do you want me to drive you home?" Jackson walked up behind him, taking him by the arm. "This way to the door."

"Thanks. And yeah, I guess it would be good if you drove."

"What are you going to do about Cheyenne?"

He kept walking. "Not sure."

He guessed he'd pray and hope that God had a plan, because he didn't have one of his own.

He hadn't had a plan when he'd married her. He sure didn't have a plan on how to keep her in his life.

They drove through Dawson pretty slowly. "Is she at the shop?"

Jackson turned, and Reese knew they were going down the side road where the barbershop was located. "Yeah, she's in there. You want out?"

"Yeah, drop me off. It's time my wife and I had a talk."

The truck stopped. Jackson stopped him from getting out. "I don't think I'd go in there with that attitude."

"Really? What would you do?"

"I think I'd come up with something a little more romantic. Just saying."

Romance. He let out a sigh. Yeah, sure. "Okay, take me out to the ranch."

"Will do."

Something romantic. Yeah, he could do romance. He didn't know if it would convince her to give them a chance, but he could definitely give romance a try.

When Jackson's truck came back an hour after the first time it had stopped out front, Cheyenne was surprised. She had drawn her own conclusions when she'd watched Jackson and Reese have a conversation earlier and then drive away. In her mind Jackson had talked Reese into leaving. Or maybe Jackson had taken Reese home to get the paperwork that they needed to sign.

She put baby Reese in the bassinet and stepped quietly away, hoping he would sleep a little while. She hadn't slept much in the past few weeks. It was not because of the baby but because she'd been missing Dawson—and Reese. Her mom had talked her into coming back here. She'd told Cheyenne that her heart seemed to be in Dawson and so maybe she should give the town and her life here a chance.

Cheyenne had agreed to staying for a month. That would give her time to see how people were going to react to the dissolution of her marriage. She knew that being married to Reese had given her an easy acceptance into this small town that she might not have otherwise had.

And ending that marriage? She didn't know what would happen to the relationships she'd built. She had decided to overlook the man who said she was just another stray that Reese Cooper brought home to take care of.

She was more than a stray. She had made a life for herself. Yes, it was with Reese's help. But surviving the past ten years she'd done on her own.

The front door opened. She stood at the back of the shop, watching as Reese walked in. Her heart leaped ahead of her, getting lost in the cowboy standing in her shop. She smiled when he took off his glasses and dropped them in his pocket. Next he took off his hat and hung it on a hook on the wall.

"Cheyenne?"

She didn't know what to say. She could tell him to leave. Maybe she should ask him to leave the paperwork for the annulment and go.

"Marco." He stepped a little farther into the room, a smile on his handsome face.

"Polo." She let out a ragged breath as he turned that smile on her and walked toward her.

"Very good. You're learning the rules of the game." He walked straight up to her. She inhaled his scent, got caught in his nearness. She shouldn't have come back, not when it was this hard being around him.

"That game is easy."

He remained in front of her. "I've missed you."

She bit down on her bottom lip and nodded. And then she answered, the reply sneaking out before she could stop it. "I missed you, too."

"Are you back in business? You know, I'm going to need a shave and a haircut soon."

"I haven't decided," she admitted, taking his hand and leading him back to the chairs at the rear of the shop. She sat in the rocking chair. He took the wingback, pulling it close before sitting.

"What's to decide?"

"I don't want to stay if people…"

"…think you've walked out on me?" He handed her a manila envelope.

"What's this?"

"The papers." He smiled. "Cheyenne, people in Dawson love you. They're going to support you no matter what."

She pulled the paper out of the envelope, her hands shaking. This was it, time to let go of someone she had, for some crazy reason, started seeing in her life forever.

The memories of that day in Vegas came back, bittersweet, taunting. They'd stood before a minister, their hands clasped in agreement, her heart pounding as the vows were recited. He'd kissed her, holding her easy in his arms. And then he'd told her that this would help her get her life back on track. He would feel better about going to Afghanistan because if something happened to him then he'd know that one really good thing had come of it.

Something had happened. He'd come home

to heal. She'd fallen in love with a man who had wanted to do one good thing with his life. And from what she could see, he'd always done good. He'd always done right. He'd even stay married to her because it was what his family called the "right thing to do."

"Cheyenne?"

She looked up from the envelope and brushed at her eyes. "I'm here. I'm sorry. Let me get a pen."

"Have you looked at the paper?"

"No," she admitted, the word not easy to say.

"Look at it."

She read it, unsure. She read it again and looked at him. He smiled, staring straight ahead.

"Reese, this is the wrong paper. This is our marriage license."

"I know." He moved from his chair, kneeling on one knee in front of her as he reached into his pocket. "Cheyenne, I'm not willing to let you go. I know that we had a deal. I'll honor that agreement if that's what you really want. But it isn't what I want."

"What do you want?"

"I want you in my life forever. I want you to pack up yourself, that little guy in there and come with me to the ranch. I want to be the man you need me to be."

"Reese, I can't do that to you. You're the most honorable man I know. I don't want to wake up someday and know that you resent me or regret us."

"Regret you?" He reached for her hand. "The only thing I regret is that we've wasted so much time pretending we don't love each other. Because I do love you, Mrs. Cooper, and unless I'm mistaken, you love me back."

She leaned, cupping his cheeks in her hands and kissing him once, and then again. "I do love you."

He reached into his pocket and held out a ring—the ruby ring that Myrna Cooper had insisted she should wear. "Cheyenne Cooper, will you marry me? Because the only regret I have is that we didn't have a real church wedding with family and a honeymoon someplace sandy with waves crashing against the shore."

"You really want to marry me?"

He stood and he pulled her up with him. "I want to marry you. I want you in my life forever, Cheyenne. I want that little boy in there to grow up at Cooper Creek. I want you to trust me when I tell you I will never regret marrying you. Not the first time, or second."

He touched her hand and then lifted it and slid the ring in place. "I love you. And marrying you that day in Vegas was the smartest thing I ever did."

He touched her cheek, touched her lips and then his mouth was on hers. He held her close and whispered that he would always love her, and then he asked her if she would agree to a second wedding at the Dawson Community Church—soon.

Reese loved her. She wanted to hold on to that moment. She wanted to stay in his arms. She thought back to that moment when she'd bumped into a cowboy coming out of the diner and how that moment had changed her life. She closed her eyes and whispered a silent thank-you because God had known she needed this cowboy, that they needed each other.

She leaned into his shoulder. "Yes, Reese. I'll marry you."

Epilogue

Cheyenne stood at the back of the church, comparing this wedding to the wedding in Vegas. This time her dad stood next to her. Her sister and Heather were already walking down the aisle as her bridesmaids. At the front of the church Reese waited. He faced the back of the church, and she knew a groom had never loved a bride as much as he loved her. The thought rushed through her and she smiled, wishing he could see her smile, see the love in her eyes. But she knew he felt it.

He sensed it.

As beautiful as their autumn wedding would be, she would always cherish the Vegas wedding. Here she had flowers, people who loved them and wanted to witness their vows. In Vegas they'd taken a chance and God had done something wonderful.

"Are you ready?" Her dad placed her hand on his arm.

"More than ready."

Reese Cooper had been her husband for almost a year when she walked down the aisle on the arm of her father. At that first ceremony she had married a stranger she thought she'd never see again. Today she took the same vows, but today he was the man she loved with all of her heart. And she knew that he loved her as deeply.

They were no longer strangers bound by a commitment. They were husband and wife— and son. To unite them as one, Heather handed her baby Reese. Cheyenne took her son in one arm and Reese held her other hand.

Wyatt Johnson prayed at the end of the ceremony, and she closed her eyes and said a silent thank-You to God, because He had known they would need each other.

"I now pronounce you husband and wife," Wyatt smiled and proclaimed, "You may kiss your bride. Again."

Heather took the baby and stepped back.

Reese turned and drew her into his arms. As he kissed her wildly in front of the cheering congregation, she laughed and cried and kissed him wildly back.

"Save it for the honeymoon," Jackson whispered as he walked away from his position as best man.

Cheyenne smiled as her husband kissed her again.

"I love you, Mrs. Cooper."

* * * * *

Look for Brenda Minton's next
COOPER CREEK novel,
available in February 2013
from Love Inspired Books.

Dear Reader,

Welcome back to Dawson, Oklahoma. This is the third book in the Cooper Creek series, and I hope you're enjoying getting to know the Cooper family. The hero of *The Rancher's Secret Wife* is cowboy Reese Cooper. From the beginning, Reese has been the good guy. In past stories, he showed up to help his neighbors, his family, his friends. It only made sense that a guy like Reese would want to defend his country. It also made sense to me that Reese would want to rescue a woman like Cheyenne Jones. He would want to give her a chance because he's always had so much.

Reese is a hero, but a fictional hero. The true heroes and heroines are the men and women who serve this country daily. They leave behind the homes, the farms, the families that they love. They sacrifice for the greater good of a nation. I hope that Reese Cooper portrays those men and women. If you see a soldier, tell them "thank you" for their service. Show them that their nation is grateful and appreciates the sacrifices that they make.

Brenda Minton

Questions for Discussion

1. When Cheyenne shows up in Dawson, she believes she is just there to make sure Reese Cooper is okay. Do you think she might have hoped Reese would accept her into his life as something more than a temporary arrangement?

2. Reese doesn't immediately tell his family who Cheyenne is. Why would he not tell them? What would you do in similar circumstances?

3. In the beginning, what do you think attracts Cheyenne to Dawson? Is it the small-town life or is it Reese who keeps her there?

4. Are you surprised by how Reese's family accepts Cheyenne? What reaction would you expect them to have?

5. Reese loses his eyesight in a combat situation. How would you deal with something that traumatic? How do you think Reese handles his loss?

6. Reese suffers from PTSD and flashbacks. Both are difficult situations that people

don't always understand or know how to deal with. Added to the loss of vision, does it make sense that he would hold back from Cheyenne?

7. How do you think Cheyenne helps Reese, who really seems to be strong enough on his own?

8. Why do you think it was important for Reese to meet the Bernards, the couple who lost a son in the same incident where Reese lost his eyesight?

9. Cheyenne's parents adopted her because they thought they couldn't have biological children. Later, they do conceive and have a daughter. How does that change their relationship with Cheyenne?

10. As parents, we don't always make the right decisions for our children. Sometimes our reactions are wrong. What do you think went wrong in the relationship between Cheyenne and her parents?

11. The Bible tells us not to let the sun go down on our anger. How could that principle help us in situations such as Cheyenne's, where

there seemed to be a lot of miscommunication? Why is communication important in all relationships?

12. When do you think Cheyenne and Reese really started falling in love? What situation changes how they feel about ending their marriage?

13. Reese has some doubts as to whether or not he can take care of Cheyenne while still learning to take care of himself. Does he have a valid point or concern?

14. Does it make sense that Cheyenne doesn't want to feel as if she trapped Reese into a relationship that he thought would be temporary?

LARGER-PRINT BOOKS!

**GET 2 FREE
LARGER-PRINT NOVELS
PLUS 2 FREE
MYSTERY GIFTS**

Love Inspired

Larger-print novels are now available...

LILP11B

Love Inspired®
SUSPENSE
RIVETING INSPIRATIONAL ROMANCE

Watch for our series of edge-
of-your-seat suspense novels.
These contemporary tales
of intrigue and romance
feature Christian characters
facing challenges to their faith...
and their lives!

AVAILABLE IN REGULAR
& LARGER-PRINT FORMATS

For exciting stories that reflect traditional values,
visit:
www.ReaderService.com